AGAINST ANOTHER MACHINE, HUMAN PROVES NOTHING, THE ROBOT SAID.

With its one arm it picked up a fencing épée and threw it to Hosato, who caught it easily.

"You have an unbroken record of success, a long line of dead men behind you," the metallic voice grated. "Then let this be your last challenge: Match your mind and abilities against mine—against a robot!"

Before Hosato could launch an attack, however, it quickly snatched up a second sword and had it between them. Hosato extended his épée and settled into an *en garde* position. The robot knew him too well. He'd rather be killed in a fight than go meekly to the slaughter.

And he wanted to prove, even with his dying breath, that he could beat it, that a man was better than a machine.

MIRROR FRIEND, MIRROR FOE

A TALE OF HIGH ADVENTURE
IN THE FARTHEST REACHES OF SPACE BY
ROBERT ASPRIN
(creator of <u>Thieves' World</u>™)
and **GEORGE TAKEI**
("Sulu" of <u>Star Trek</u>)

ROBERT ASPRIN & GEORGE TAKEI
Mirror Friend, Mirror Foe

ACE SCIENCE FICTION BOOKS
NEW YORK

MIRROR FRIEND, MIRROR FOE

An Ace Science Fiction Book / published by arrangement with
the authors

PRINTING HISTORY
Playboy edition / December 1979
Third printing / September 1980
Ace edition / December 1985

ISBN: 0-441-53380-9

Ace Science Fiction Books are published by The Berkley Publishing Group,
200 Madison Avenue, New York, New York 10016.
PRINTED IN THE UNITED STATES OF AMERICA

1

He would have to fight the boy. All the argument thus far had proved was that the youth had no logical objections, but was making them up as he went along to support his own stubborn streak. The only way to end the discussion would be to teach the kid a lesson —physically.

Having reached this conclusion, Hosato began to reassess the situation, specifically viewing the room as a battlefield, as he continued the discussion.

"Be reasonable, James. I've been hired to do a job, like anyone else in this complex. That job is to teach you how to fence. It wasn't my idea, it was your father's, so instead of arguing, let's get on with the job at hand."

"But I don't want to learn to fence!" the boy insisted, his gray eyes glowering from beneath a sandy tousle of hair.

"Why not?"

The boy was tall, in his mid-teens, and broad for his age. He'd have the advantage of reach, since Hosato barely came up to his shoulders in height, but whatever edge his youth gave him in speed should be offset by his awkwardness.

"It's silly," the boy grumbled. "Why should I waste my time learning something I'll never use? Swords are obsolete . . . so are guns, for that matter, but at least a gun would train me for using a blaster."

"Are you carrying a gun or a blaster at the moment?" Hosato inquired politely.

"No," James admitted. "You aren't allowed to

carry an energy weapon inside the complex . . . unless you're a security guard."

"But you *are* wearing a sword."

From what Hosato could see, the boy's sword had a slender blade roughly one meter long. The overly ornate hilt indicated it was more a decoration than a functional weapon. Probably no cutting edges, which would restrict his opponent to attacking with the point.

"Of course I'm wearing a sword. Anyone of any station worth mentioning does."

"But you can't see any reason for learning to use it?"

The boy's beige cotton-and-nylon jumpsuit would give him freedom of movement, though not as much as Hosato's black fencing uniform. The soft-soled boots would give him traction, but the cloak was too long. With any luck, he'd trip over that cloak, or at least find it tangling his arm if he turned too suddenly.

"No, I don't," the youth retorted. "Nobody actually fights with swords. They're a fashionable status symbol. Two years ago it was spangle gloves, today it's swords. Big deal."

Hosato abandoned his preparatory observations to make one last effort to convince the boy logically.

"Look, James. Your father is one of the most important men in this complex—a complex, I might add, that is constantly feuding with another complex on Grünbecker's planet. That makes you a prime target for kidnapping or assassination. Realizing that, can't you see the value of learning to use the one weapon the laws let you carry?"

"Let Security handle them." The boy shrugged. "That's what we pay them for."

The tile floor of the rec room would give them decent footing, though not ideal. The far end of the room was still in darkness, but the X aisle between the four pool tables would be well lighted enough to work in. Having completed his survey, Hosato moved to set up the confrontation.

"Security will handle them." He sneered, mimicking the boy's voice. "And what if they don't? What will you do then? File a complaint? Or would you be forced to do your own fighting for a change?"

The main vulnerability of youth is not inexperience, it's pride. The boy's head came up with a snap as he reacted to the slight.

"I can take care of myself if I have to."

"Is that a fact?" Hosato stung the boy with a patronizing smile. "Tell you what, James. If I can prove to you that you can't handle yourself in a fight, will you agree to study what I have to teach you?"

"That wouldn't be fair," the youth protested. "I didn't say I could cross swords with a fencing master and win. But there aren't that many fencing masters around. I can hold my own against the kind of opponent I'd be likely to have to fight, though."

Hosato smiled. "It seems there are a few misconceptions here we should clear up. First of all, I'm not a fencing master. I'm a professional duelist. I'm supposed to teach you to fight, not score points in a tournament. Second . . ."—he showed a few more teeth— "I didn't say I'd cross swords with you. I'm betting you're sloppy enough with that weapon I could defend myself without using a sword."

The boy started to reply angrily, but caught himself.

"No deal," he said suspiciously. "You'll probably use karate or something."

"As a matter of fact, I don't know karate," Hosato lied easily.

"Why not?" asked the boy. "I mean, you're Oriental."

"That's right. I can't use chopsticks, either."

Hosato caught himself before his annoyance grew. The boy had inadvertently touched a nerve, but it wouldn't do to go into this fight mad.

"We're getting off the subject. I'm proposing a little contest. You use a sword, and I don't. If you can draw blood on me in five minutes, I'll go to your father and tell him you don't need lessons. Is it a deal?"

The boy hesitated. "What if I kill you?" he asked.

"Then I'll be dead and you won't have to take lessons."

"I mean, what would I tell my father? With you dead, there'd be no one to say it was an exercise. I'd look like a murderer."

Hosato smiled to himself. The boy was bright enough. Maybe he'd make a fencer after all.

"Don't worry about it, James," he said confidently. Hosato pulled a small flat box from where it was clipped inside his tunic. He thumbed a dial and lifted the unit to his lips.

"Suzi!" he said.

From the depths of the darkened end of the rec room came the whir of small high-speed motors, and a strange shape emerged into the light.

It was obviously a robot, but a very specialized robot. It stood six feet high, floating on a cushion of air, and was shaped like a rectangular metal box stood on end. One side was a rough manikin form, and had a jointed mechanical arm dangling from it.

"Meet Suzi," Hosato said. "My combination equipment closet and fencing assistant."

"So what?" said the youth, unimpressed.

Hosato spoke into the control box again. "Suzi! Display replay camera three . . . two minutes back."

In response, the machine pivoted about to reveal a viewscreen mounted on the end opposite the arm. A picture sprang into focus, of Hosato and James in conversation.

". . . draw blood on me in five minutes, I'll go to your father—"

"Stop, Suzi!" Hosato turned to the boy. "There's your witness."

The youth was craning his neck to peer around the room.

"Have you got cameras in here?" he asked.

"Yes. I tape all my lessons," Hosato replied. "They're spaced around the room to make sure the action is captured from all angles."

He pointed to a small black box no bigger than a matchbox, perched on the pool table by the boy's elbow.

"How many cameras are there, Hayama?" a new voice inquired, using Hosato's alias. It came to them from the other end of the room as a new figure stepped into view.

Sasha! Hosato frowned to himself as he recognized the svelte figure of the security chief. He was going to have trouble with this lady. She was too efficient and moved a bit too quietly for his comfort.

"Half a dozen," he answered, forcing a smile. "I didn't see you come in."

"You weren't supposed to," she replied without smiling. "Go ahead, Master James. I'll be your witness that you attacked your teacher at his own request." She draped herself casually over a folding chair next to the robot.

James looked uncomfortable for a moment, then grudgingly drew his sword. Hosato felt a quick wave of sympathy for the boy. He had run out of excuses and was now forced into doing combat with a fencing coach in front of an attractive woman. To say the least, it was an unenviable position.

Reluctantly the boy raised his sword into an awkward initiation of an *en garde* position.

Instead of responding in kind, Hosato simply stood facing him squarely, arms folded across his chest. They watched each other intently for a few moments; then Hosato cocked an expectant eyebrow.

The youth, suddenly realizing Hosato wasn't going to do anything more in preparation, began to edge cautiously forward. Hosato remained motionless. Finally the boy screwed up his courage and poked his sword forward in a quick jab.

Without moving his hands, Hosato stepped leisurely backward, and the attack fell short.

He continued sauntering backward, and raised the control box to his lips once more. "Suzi!" he said loudly. "Give us a buzzer in five minutes, starting . . . now!"

Tucking the box back inside his tunic, he reversed his field and approached the boy once more.

"Okay, James," he said in a barely audible murmur. "Try it again, and this time act as if you mean it. We've got an audience!"

The boy flushed and sprang forward, not waiting for Hosato to stop moving. The blade darted toward his tormentor's chest, but encountered only thin air. The target disappeared as Hosato pulled his left shoulder back, twisting his torso parallel to the advancing blade. The point passed harmlessly by, scant inches from his chest.

"Much better!" he said, retreating easily up one of the aisles. "A few more like that and I'll have to start treating you seriously."

The boy pressed forward, on the attack again, only to find Hosato had changed his track. He was standing sideways now, his right hand extended leisurely, as if holding an invisible sword.

Puzzled, the boy jabbed at the hand . . . and missed again as the hand drifted back to its original position. Annoyed now, the boy stepped forward and tried to thrust past the hand at Hosato's body. The blade was batted disdainfully aside by the hand that now seemed to be blocking the path of attack.

Hosato drifted sideways, putting the pool table between himself and the stalking youth. The boy paralleled his motion, sword extended over the width of the table, watching Hosato's movements as a lynx watches a rabbit. Again he jabbed with the sword, only to find he had again misjudged the distance.

Hosato moved neither foot nor hand in defense, laughing at the boy's frustration as the pool table brought his attack up short.

Suddenly the control box inside Hosato's tunic started to tingle against his body. He risked a glance over his shoulder. Sasha was standing with her back to them, closely examining the robot.

There was a flash of movement in the corner of his eye, and Hosato snapped his attention back to the fight. Too late! During his moment of distraction, the boy had slipped around the end of the pool table and was sprinting at his tormentor with his sword at full extension.

Hosato was caught flatfooted. The sword point was scant inches from his body and there was no way he could defend himself—legitimately.

Reflex action took over. Hosato dropped to the floor under the speeding sword point. As he did, his foot lashed out in a vicious kick. In that flashing moment, his conscious mind regained partial control . . . but not in time. He checked the main force of the kick and moved the point of impact from the diaphragm to the stomach, but that was all he could do.

The kick landed, and the boy doubled over and collapsed on the floor. The sword slipped from his fingers and clattered noisily away as he gasped for breath.

Hosato rippled to his feet and was at the boy's side in an eye blink. "Are you all right, James?" he asked, lifting the youth by his armpits to aid his breathing.

All the while, he was cursing reflexes—his reflexes and his inattentiveness. To give himself away this early in the game . . .

"What happened?" demanded Sasha, standing beside them.

"He . . . he kicked me!" the boy gasped.

"Nonsense!" Hosato snapped indignantly. "The boy got overenthusiastic and ran into the corner of the table there. Knocked the wind out of him."

"You said you wouldn't use karate!" the boy whined accusingly, ignoring Hosato's protest.

"I told you I don't know any karate!"

"This can be settled easily enough," Sasha interrupted. "Let's see the replay on your cameras, Hayama."

Her voice was casual, but her eyes were studying Hosato with soft suspicion.

"An excellent suggestion," Hosato said, fishing the control box out of his tunic. "Suzi! Camera five. Display replay. One minute back."

The viewscreen winked obediently to life, and two figures swam into focus. Hosato waited, poised, as James circled wide around one end of the pool table . . . the boy darted forward . . . Hosato floated lightly behind the table again . . . James tried to change his course, slammed into the corner of the table, doubled over, and rolled off onto the the floor. . . .

"Interrupt, Suzi!" Hosato ordered.

The screen went dark again.

"You see? The boy just—"

A raucous buzzer went off in the robot.

"What was that?" Sasha demanded.

"The signal that five minutes is up. I forgot to cancel the timing order."

Sasha ignored his answer and turned to the boy again. "Well, James? Was that what happened?"

The boy was still sitting on the floor staring thoughtfully at the dark viewscreen.

"Huh? Oh! Yeah, Sasha. I forgot about the cameras. I was just trying to get out of taking fencing lessons."

Now it was the boy's turn to suffer the security chief's piercing study.

"In that case, I think you owe Hayama here an apology."

James lurched shakily to his feet and extended his hand.

"I'm sorry, Hayama. All things considered, I've

changed my mind. I'd like to take those lessons, if you'll have me as a student."

The boy had given up too easily. There was a new depth in his gaze that hadn't been there when they first met.

"Certainly I'll have you, James," Hosato said, accepting the handshake. "If anything, I should apologize to you for putting you through such a rough first lesson."

The boy picked up his sword and resheathed it.

"If it's all right," he said, "I think I'll go lie down for a while. I'm still a little queasy from that . . . accident."

"Go ahead." Hosato smiled. "Same time tomorrow?"

"Right."

"Wait outside a minute, James," interjected Sasha. "I'll walk along with you."

The boy hesitated, then nodded and left.

"We'll have to have dinner together, Hayama. Sometime soon?"

Sasha's smile didn't reach her eyes. Hosato ignored the warning bells going off in the back of his mind.

"Sure, Sasha," he said, forcing a smile. "Any particular reason?"

"Nothing special. You're the newest person on the staff, and I know the least about you. I thought it might give us a chance to get to know each other better."

"I thought those application forms I filled out were pretty complete."

Sasha smiled as if at some secret joke. "Forms seldom tell the whole story."

"Well, how about tonight, then?"

"There's no hurry. No one leaves the complex without my approval."

She turned and followed James before Hosato could reply, which was fortunate, because he couldn't think of one. He stared about the twosome for a few moments, then thoughtfully began to collect his remote cameras.

"Suspicious bitch!" said Suzi.

Involuntarily Hosato shot a darting glance around the room. "Someone might be listening, you know," he said.

"Sensors detect no human or electronic surveillance," the robot retorted.

Hosato grimaced. He should know by now the futility of arguing with his partner.

"Come on, Suzi. Give me a hand with these cameras."

The robot floated over to him, but would not be distracted from her observations.

"They're both suspicious, you know. The security chief *and* the boy."

"I know, Suzi."

"Don't underestimate the security chief just because she's a female."

"If anything, I'm tracking her doubly close because she's a female, Suzi."

"I thought so!" The robot sniffed haughtily.

Hosato secured the last camera in the storage compartment and began unfastening his tunic. As he did, the door of the compartment slid shut, then reopened, exposing an entirely different storage area.

"I wish you'd use the normal doors when we're on assignment," Hosato commented. "It's supposed to be a secret that you can rearrange your internals."

"It *is* a secret," the robot retorted. "I told you, no one's watching."

Hosato ignored the rebuff. His attention was devoted instead to the two swords displayed in this compartment. The dueling épées! No matter how often he saw them—whether as a student or after the maestro had presented them to him—they always gave him a vague chill.

The swords had been used over the centuries for sixty-three bloodings and thirty-one kills. A total of ninety-four duels—no, make that ninety-five. He had forgotten to include the latest duel, the one that immediately preceded this contract. . . .

ꙅꙅꙅꙅꙅꙅꙅꙅꙅꙅ **2** ꙅꙅꙅꙅꙅꙅꙅꙅꙅꙅ

It had all started on Mitchum's planet . . . There were four of them waiting by the designated rock. Even though they were still in sight of the spaceport, no crowd gathered to watch. Apparently duels such as this were not uncommon.

Hosato studied the group as he approached them. Suzi floated silently at his side, her disapproval displayed by the absence of her traditional comments and observations.

Three of the men were obviously the Seale brothers. Their flashy, stylish clothes disguised neither the family resemblance nor the arrogant slouch of habitual bar toughs. They were long-limbed and broad-shouldered; their build and manner set them apart from the fourth man, even more than their obvious difference in color.

The fourth man stood slightly apart from the others. He was bald and Negroid, his ramrod-stiff posture marking him as military. His face was impassive, but his well-muscled, compact body and poised readiness were enough to cause anyone to give him wide berth. It was obvious to the most casual observer that the worn holster of his blaster had not been purchased used, but had aged the hard way.

The bald man moved forward to meet Hosato. "Mr. Mathers?" he asked.

"I am Hayama," said Hosato. "I have been retained by Mr. Mathers to settle this affair."

The bald man swept him with a speculative glance before replying. "I am Moabe, Mr. Hayama. I have been asked to serve as umpire."

Hosato inclined his head slightly in formal acknowledgment.

"Hey! Are you one of Mathers' seconds?"

Hosato turned to face the speaker. "Might I ask whom I am addressing?" he queried.

"I'm Harry Seale, the challenger. These are my brothers, Casey and Tom."

Hosato inclined his head to them. "I am Hayama."

One of the brothers, Tom, snorted derisively. The other studied Hosato carefully.

"You didn't answer Brother Harry's question," he commented quietly.

"I have been retained by Mr. Mathers to settle this affair," Hosato replied. "He sends his regrets over last night's incident and states he is ready to make public apology under any condition you might set forth."

Tom grinned and began making clucking noises like a chicken.

Harry was more to the point. "No deal, Hayama. He's not getting off the hook that easy. I challenged him and he accepted, so he's going to have to fight. You just go back and tell him we'll wait here one more hour. If he isn't here by then, we'll come and get him."

Hosato smiled. "That will not be necessary. As I said, I have been instructed by Mr. Mathers to settle the affair. If possible, this was to be done with an apology. If not . . ." He shrugged and let the sentence hang in the air.

"What do you mean—?" Harry began.

"He's taking Mathers' place," interrupted Casey.

"What?" exploded Tom, finally coming to life. "He can't do that! Mathers was challenged, and he's got to be the one to fight."

Hosato looked at the umpire.

"It is not without precedent," Moabe ruled, "for a challenged party to appoint a champion to fight in his stead."

The brothers bit off their objections and huddled together for a quick conference.

Hosato smiled to himself. He found a certain ironic justice in the situation. If thugs tried to use the format of a duel to cloak a murder, it was only fitting they find themselves bound by the rules and traditions governing that form of combat. He caught Moabe's eye. The black looked at him impassively for a moment, then slowly closed one eye in a conspiratorial wink. Hosato was not the only one present who appreciated the humor of the situation.

"Okay, Hayama!" Harry called. The huddle was breaking up. "It's your funeral. If you want to die instead of Mathers, that's your privilege. We're willing to settle this with you."

Moabe was suddenly between them, one hand on the butt of his blaster.

"A duel is individual combat," he said levelly. "The seconds are to serve as witnesses only, and are not to take an active part in the battle."

"Hey, Moabe!" Tom protested. "Remember, we're the ones who are paying you."

"That's right," Moabe retorted, "and you're paying me to umpire this duel, which means I guarantee the rules are strictly followed by *both* sides."

"Shut up, Tom!" Casey interrupted. "Don't worry, Moabe. This is Harry's fight. He'd probably shoot us himself if we interfered."

His smile was not convincing.

"Very well, gentlemen," Hosato replied, as if there had been no interruption. "As repesentative of the challenged party, I believe I have choice of weapons. I choose épées."

"What?" bellowed Harry.

"Epées," said Moabe. "Swords. Not only is it an acceptable dueling weapon, it is one of the original dueling weapons."

"Go ahead, Harry," called Casey. "It's like using a long knife."

"But I don't have a sword," protested Harry.

Hosato was already at Suzi's side, opening one of her many storage compartments.

"I happen to have a matched set of dueling épées.

Mr. Moabe, if you would be so good as to inspect them for acceptability . . . ?"

He passed the weapons to Moabe, who examined them closely. The Negro's eyebrows shot up with surprised appreciation before he caught himself and restored his normal unmoved expression.

"Yes. These weapons are acceptable," he ruled. "Mr. Seale, as your opponent has provided the weapons, you have first choice."

He offered both weapons to Harry, who scowled suspiciously, then made a large show of examining them closely before choosing.

"My client will accept first blood in settling this matter," Hosato announced.

"What's that supposed to mean?" Tom demanded.

"Duels may be settled by first, second, or third blood," Moabe informed him. "First blood means just that—the duel is ended when blood is drawn, however trivial. Second blood means the duel will be fought to the first serious injury. Third blood is a duel to the death, and the fight will continue until one of the combatants is dead, even if it means the seconds have to hold a wounded duelist up until the death blow is struck."

"Oh!" said Tom, properly mollified.

Casey had been studying Hosato suspiciously throughout the exchange. "You seem to know an awful lot about this stuff, Hayama," he commented.

"This is not my first duel," Hosato admitted.

"Hayama!" Harry exploded in sudden recognition. "Hey! I've heard of you! You're a professional duelist!"

Hosato inclined his head in acknowledgment. There was a pregnant moment of silence as the brothers exchanged glances.

"Mr. Seale," said Moabe, stepping forward, "do you wish to reconsider accepting Mr. Mathers' apology?"

Harry started, then brandished his sword. "Why?

I'm not scared of him. Come on, Hayama. Let's get this thing over with."

Mentally, Hosato cursed Moabe. If he had just kept his mouth shut for a few more minutes, Harry might have backed down on his own. But Harry was a bully, and would never back away from a fight on someone else's suggestion. Well, there was no getting out of it now. With a sigh Hosato stepped forward and struck a pose, legs straight, sword and sword arm extended level at shoulder height.

Harry regarded the stance suspiciously.

"If you will come *en garde,* Mr. Seale," Moabe prompted. "Extend your sword until its point touches that of Mr. Hayama's. I will then give the signal to begin."

Harry shot a black look at the umpire, then awkwardly initiated Hosato's stance and extended his sword.

"Ready, gentlemen? Fighting for first blood. Begin!"

It was over almost before it started. Harry plunged forward, trying to overwhelm and surprise his opponent, but he made a mistake. Like most novices, he ignored his opponent's arm and tried to attack deep, going for a body hit. As he closed the distance, Hosato's sword point floated out and plunged deep into the bicep of his sword arm.

Harry recoiled, dropping the sword and grasping his wounded arm.

"Halt!" called Moabe.

Hosato stepped back and relaxed his guard.

"First blood has been drawn," Moabe intoned. "The matter is settled."

"Not so fast!"

All heads turned toward the source of the voice. During the skirmish, Casey had drifted back and taken up a position behind Moabe. He was there now, but his blaster was out and leveled at the umpire.

"Harry didn't agree to this first-blood bull."

"He entered into combat after the terms had—"

"Shut up, Moabe! What do you say, Harry?"

"Come on, Casey. I'm hurt!"

Casey glared at his brother for a moment, then turned his gaze to Hosato. "Hayama," he said, "I know you wouldn't want to take advantage of Harry's condition, so what say you switch that sword over to your left hand. Now!"

Slowly Hosato complied with the order.

"Okay now, Harry?" Casey called.

"Okay! Come on, Hayama. Just you and me."

Hosato advanced slowly to meet him.

Harry was lying. It wasn't just the two of them. It was becoming increasingly apparent to Hosato that if he succeeded in killing Harry, one of the other brothers would gun him down, rules or no rules. He had been afraid something like this would happen. That's why he had a small, flat two-shot blaster secreted in his pocket. Casey had timed his move well, however, and there was no way to reach the weapon without drawing fire from the other two brothers.

Harry plunged forward again. Hosato parried and bounded backward, ignoring his chance for a fatal riposte.

"Not so good with your left hand, are you, Hayama?" Harry sneered.

"Get him, Harry!" Tom called from the side.

As a matter of fact, Hosato was almost as good with his left hand as he was with his right, but he didn't dare act. Tom's shout fixed the third brother's location in his mind, though, and gave him the germ of an idea.

Steeling himself, Hosato darted forward, on the attack. Harry batted the lunge clumsily aside, but didn't attempt a counterthrust as Hosato slipped past him.

"Pretty fancy, Hayama," he admitted grudgingly.

Hosato mentally heaved a sigh of relief. The move had been risky. If Harry had been an experienced fencer, he wouldn't have dared try it for fear of the reflexive counterthrust. But he had gambled, and it worked. Now he was in position. Harry advanced again, but this time Hosato gave ground, backpedaling away from his opponent.

"Ready, Moabe?" he called.

"Ready for what?" Tom demanded.

For a reply, Hosato whirled and plunged his épée into Tom's chest.

"Hey!" shouted Casey.

That was all the distraction Moabe needed. Dropping to the ground and drawing his blaster in one smooth motion, he cut Casey down with one shot.

Harry had dropped his sword and was drawing his own blaster as Casey fell. "You bastard!" he screamed, leveling the weapon at Moabe's back.

Hosato's shot took him as he squeezed the trigger stud, the two blasts sounding as one.

Silence echoed over the field.

"Moabe?" Hosato called at last.

"He has ceased to function," Suzi informed him.

Hosato hung his head in fatigue and sorrow. He had liked Moabe, however short their acquaintance had been.

Suzi retrieved Harry's sword and floated silently to his side. Hosato sighed and began to secure the weapons in her storage compartment. He didn't chide Suzi for not assisting in the fight. However human she seemed at times, she was still a robot, and therefore incapable of killing or injuring a human.

"Someone's coming," Suzi announced.

Hosato raised his head and saw a man approaching from the spaceport. This man was of a different cut than most, his conservative clothes, like a uniform, identifying him as a corporation man. He gave the strewn bodies no more than a casual glance, striding purposefully toward the survivor.

Hosato studied him with mild curiosity as he approached. He had been hired as a duelist by corporate men before, but not often.

The man came to a halt at a slight distance. "May I ask whom I am addressing?" he inquired.

"I am Hayama," Hosato replied.

A vague ripple of relief crossed the man's face. "Excellent. My name is Reilly. I represent the Ravensteel Corporation, and we are interested in retaining your services."

Hosato's eyebrows went up. "Am I to understand it would be the corporation and not yourself individually who would be retaining my skills?"

"That's right. Why? Is something wrong?"

"No. I just can't imagine why a corporation would require the services of a duelist."

"We don't." Reilly smiled. "You see, we at Ravensteel are aware that despite your obvious abilities, dueling is not your main livelihood, just as Hayama isn't your real name. Your name is Hosato, and you are a free-lance spy and saboteur—one of the best, according to our sources. Ravensteel needs a saboteur, and we need one badly. The fact you can fence is merely frosting on the cake."

3

"Mr. Mathers?"

The bartender turned at the sound of Hosato's voice. "Hayama!" he exclaimed.

"It is settled," Hosato said quietly.

"They accepted my apology?"

"No."

"But you said . . . Oh."

"Harry Seale will not trouble you again. Neither will his two brothers."

Mathers stood regarding Hosato with a new respect.

"I see. Well, I guess you want the rest of your money."

He went to the cash register, and returned with a handful of bills. Wordlessly he counted them onto the bar counter in front of Hosato.

Hosato picked them up without checking the count and started to stash them in his tunic; then he hesitated. "Did you know Moabe?" he asked.

"The Negro. No, I didn't know him and didn't want to. The Seales always had a couple darkies hanging around with them. Never could warm up to them, myself."

"I see," said Hosato.

"Hey, nothing personal, you understand. You Orientals are all right. You're quiet and polite. But Negroes . . . well . . . you know how they are."

Mathers smiled and winked knowingly.

Hosato regarded him for a moment, then put away the money and turned to leave.

"Hey! No need to hurry off, Hayama. Come on,

I'll buy you a drink. I figure I owe you a little bonus."

Hosato left without acknowledging Mathers' words.

Reilly was waiting in his hotel room as promised, and answered the door promptly when Hosato knocked.

"Come in, come in," he invited. "I hope you don't mind meeting in my room, but I thought it would be best if we weren't seen together in public."

"It's quite all right," Hosato assured him.

"Well, make yourself comfortable. Can I get you something to drink?"

"Not just now, thanks."

After the abortive duel, Hosato wanted a drink badly, but thought it unwise to drink if business were to be discussed. He seated himself on the plush sofa and waited while Reilly poured himself a healthy glass of Scotch. He wished he could have brought Suzi along, but it would have been too hard to explain her presence and might have aroused suspicions as to her true capacities.

"You sure I can't get you anything?" Reilly asked, smiling. He was obviously back in his own element again. The stiffness and formality he had displayed at the dueling ground disappeared now that he was in a hotel room with a drink in his hand.

Hosato had encountered his kind before. An aging pretty boy . . . sincere smile and a firm handshake . . . look you right in the eye: the trademark of a corporate field man. Hosato never really felt at ease around them. He preferred the company of the rougher set, who would throw back their heads and laugh or glare with suspicion. The unshakable joviality of the corporation types was a mask that successfully screened their true thoughts and reactions.

"Well, I guess you must have a million questions, Mr. Hosato," Reilly said, pulling up a chair.

"For the moment, just one." Hosato smiled. "Who gave you my name?"

"Oh, that. A gentleman called the 'Hungarian' referred us to you."

The Hungarian! That gave a certain air of credibility to the contact. Still . . .

"Did he send any messages to me?" Hosato asked.

"As a matter of fact, he did. I was going to mention it later, since it didn't seem particularly important. He said to tell you his dog died."

That was the fail-safe. The Hungarian never owned a dog in his life; in fact, he hated them. However, it served to confirm that Reilly had indeed been checked and forwarded by the Hungarian.

"Very well, tell me about this job you have for me. You mentioned sabatoge?"

"That's right," Reilly confirmed. "What do you know about Ravensteel Inc. and McCrae Enterprises?"

"Not much," Hosato admitted. "They're both based on Grünbecker's Planet and they both make robots."

Reilly smiled. "Mr. Hosato, you have an unsuspected talent for understatement. Still, that pretty much sums up the situation. The only major amendment I would make would be to point out that between the two of them, they produce eighty-five to ninety percent of the robots in use today."

Hosato raised his eyebrows in genuine surprise. He had no idea those two corporations dominated the industry to that extent.

"Now, then," Reilly continued, "what do you know about the corporations themselves, particularly their interrelation with each other?"

"Mr. Reilly"—Hosato smiled to hide his annoyance—"you asked once what I knew about the corporations in question, and I told you. Now, why don't you just tell me whatever you feel is important, instead of playing Twenty Questions?"

Reilly took the rebuff smoothly.

"Sorry," he apologized. "My basic background is in marketing and sales—you know, 'get the customer involved'? Guess I've never really gotten over it.

"Well, to keep a long story short, the two corporations hate each other with a passion. Now, don't mistake this for an ordinary business rivalry. That's there, too, but it's only part of the story. Originally they were all one company, IRAM, a partnership. The two partners had a falling-out, and they split the company, forming two separate corporations. The main drive of each of the two has been to put the other out of business. So far, though, they're about even."

"What does all this have to do with me?" Hosato asked.

"We at Ravensteel want you to penetrate the McCrae complex and sabatoge their works . . . shut 'em down. We're ready to pay ten thousand credits for the attempt, and an additional ten thousand for every month McCrae is inoperative, to a maximum total of a hundred thousand credits. Are you interested?"

Hosato stared thoughtfully at the wall for several minutes before answering. There was no denying a hundred thousand credits was tempting. Still . . .

"What's the law like?" he asked abruptly.

"The law?"

"The police. What kind of opposition would I be up against?"

"No police," Reilly assured him. "Grünbecker's Planet is a corporation world. There are no inhabitants other than corporation employees. Each of the two corporations makes and enforces its own laws."

"All right, then, what is McCrae law like?"

"Tight," Reilly admitted. "Tight to the point of being paranoid. They live in constant fear of industrial espionage and are determined nothing is going to get away. Half the humans in the complex are security guards, and if any of them are indifferent or careless, we haven't been able to catch 'em at it."

Hosato pursed his lips thoughtfully. "What's the physical layout?" he asked.

"Well, Grünbecker's Planet itself is pretty desolate . . . mostly sand and rock. If it wasn't for its mineral deposits, it's doubtful it would have been settled at all."

"Breathable atmosphere?"

Reilly shook his head. "No. The complex is sealed with its own life-support systems. You'd need a surface suit to survive outside the complex."

Hosato nodded absently.

"How about the complex itself?" he asked finally.

"The McCrae complex is a series of surface buildings interconnected by subterranean tunnels," Reilly recited. "The spaceport is located on top of the Administrative Building."

"All of it's above the surface?"

"All except one building. The main computer building is subterranean for temperature control and security. The rest of the complex is aboveground. We can supply you with detailed maps of the layout if you accept the job."

Hosato considered this for a few more moments.

"Okay, Reilly," he said at last. "What's the rest of it?"

"The rest of what?"

Hosato grimaced at him. "The rest of the story. There's got to be more. You've gone to a lot of trouble to find me, and you're offering top dollar for my services. Nothing you've said so far indicates a need for a specialist. There are several hundred people who could do the job for you, and do it cheaper than me—you've probably got a couple in your own corporation. Now, assuming Ravensteel isn't in the habit of tossing away money on overqualified personnel, there's something you haven't told me—something that will make me effective where your randomly picked demolition man would fail. I want to know what that something is before I decide whether to accept or reject your offer."

Reilly took a slow sip of his drink before replying.

"All right, Hosato. I'll put all our cards on the table. McCrae's security is tight . . . and I mean really tight. They're very careful about who they let wander around their complex. Oh, they cater to tour groups, but passing visitors never get near anything vital. We think the only machines they see are do-nothing dummies rigged for show only."

"What makes you think that?" Hosato asked.

Reilly smiled. "Because that's what we do with tour groups at Ravensteel."

"I see." Hosato mentally filed away that piece of information for possible future use.

"Anyway," Reilly continued, "the only ones who get into the depths of the complex are permanent employees. And most of the designing, manufacturing, and mining are automated, so they don't hire many humans. Consequently, the ones they do hire are screened very carefully. New employees aren't simply interviewed when they appear, they're researched and then approached. Naturally, this makes infiltration a bit difficult."

"Now, the other shoe," Hosato prompted. "How am I supposed to break this airtight defense?"

"Like everyone else, they'll bend the rules for a specialist. We've gotten information that one of the McCrae executives is looking for a fencing master for his son. It was a long shot, but we figured if we could find a fencer with other . . . shall we say 'special talents,' he might be willing to listen to a proposal from us. We started searching and found you."

Hosato thought it through. It made sense. Fencing was an ability that couldn't be faked or learned overnight. You either could or you couldn't.

"We're not really throwing you to the wolves," Reilly added hastily. Apparently he mistook Hosato's silence for hesitancy.

"We're ready to provide you with a cover. We've begun creating a character, Samuel Hu. If you accept the assignment, we'll plant the appropriate documents to support your credentials and bribe the proper personal references so that when you arrive on-planet you'll have no problem clearing their security check."

Hosato shook his head. "That won't do at all," he said flatly.

"Why not?"

"For one thing, Hu is a Chinese name."

"So?" Reilly asked blankly.

"I'm Japanese . . . well, of Japanese descent."

"That's no problem." Reilly shrugged. "I'm sure I wouldn't know the difference. Nothing personal, but most people don't know the difference between the various Orientals."

Hosato decided to abandon that particular point of argument. "It still won't work," he insisted. "The kind of personal reference I would need couldn't be bought. Even if you found a fencing master who would sell an endorsement, all that would mean would be that for the right price he could be convinced to change his story or simply blow the whistle."

"So you won't do it," Reilly said, crestfallen.

Hosato smiled. "I didn't say that," he corrected. "What I said was, I wouldn't use your cover. I'll use my own. My family spent considerable time building my cover—several generations, in fact." In actuality, Hosato's family had been in "the business" nearly seven hundred years now, starting back on Old Earth in the 1500s. He reflexively suppressed this additional bit of data as he continued. "I think it will stand up to close scrutiny a bit better than anything Ravensteel could toss together on short notice."

"Fine." Reilly beamed. "I'm sure that will be agreeable. If it's all settled, then . . ."

Hosato held up a restraining hand. "Not quite. Your original plan to establish a cover for me would have cost Ravensteel a pretty penny. Since I'm providing my own cover, I think it's only fair that that cover money should be added to my advance fee . . . shall we say an extra fifteen thousand credits?"

As he spoke, he was thinking about his long-awaited drink. Negotiations were nearly over.

"It's a deal," said Reilly. "You drive a hard bargain. You better be worth it."

"I always give my employers satisfaction," said Hosato thinly. With that pronouncement, he gave Reilly a curt nod and left the hotel room, in search of a more suitable drinking partner.

4

"Welcome to McCrae Enterprises, the largest manufacturer of robots in the universe. I will be your guide for the tour, and am programmed to answer any questions you might have . . ."

Hosato hung back as the crowd jostled forward to snap pictures of the guide robot. It was both an amusing and an annoying habit of tourists everywhere. The guide robot was no different from any of the thousands of information robots throughout the galaxy, but the tourists would faithfully take pictures of it anyway—just as they took pictures of wastebaskets and lampposts. It seemed the only requirement for an object to be photographed was that it be located somewhere other than the tourists' home planet.

Suzi's control box, clipped to his waistband, was vibrating steadily, their prearranged signal that they were being watched. It came as no surprise to Hosato that they were under surveillance; in fact, he expected it. It was only natural that any strangers, such as tourists who had not been checked and cleared by Security, would be watched closely while they were on the premises.

He had spotted the small door off the reception area marked "Employment" as soon as they had departed the ship, but for the time being he ignored it. Instead, he loitered at the rear of the tour group, finding interest in the guide robot's oration.

What he was actually doing was performing a personal test. Covertly studying the reception area, he attempted to identify and count the security devices at work.

The wall immediately behind the guide robot was covered by a huge mirror, doubtless one-way glass. Having the robot give his talk from that location was a clever ploy to draw the crowd into position for observation. The wicker baskets holding potted plants were a common disguise for closed-circuit cameras, giving the watchers clear view of anyone at the rear of the crowd.

He recognized the arch they had entered through as a scanning device and suspected the carpet contained sniffer-sensors to detect explosives. Despite the hospitable appearance, McCrae Enterprises was tracking its visitors very carefully.

Hosato abandoned his inspection abruptly. Suzi's scanners would provide a more accurate and complete list than he could hope to accumulate on his own. Besides, if he stalled too long, it might look suspicious.

Drawing a few curious glances from the tourists, he sauntered over to the Employment door and opened it. Suzi clung to his heels as he entered, and never faltered in her warning signal that they were still being watched.

The room was dark until he stepped onto the carpet; then the automatic lights came on, revealing a small office with a desk robot centered in the floor and a door in the far wall. Nothing happened until the door closed behind him; then the desk robot came to life.

"This is the Employment Office," it announced politely. "The Employment Office is not part of the planned tour of our facilities. Please rejoin the tour group immediately. If you are unsure as to where the group is currently located, respond accordingly and I will provide directions as to how you may find them."

"I'm not interested in the tour," Hosato informed the machine. "I wish to apply for a position."

There was the whir of a small motor, and a piece of paper slid into view on the desk.

"There are no openings at present in McCrae Enterprises," the machine informed him. "If you wish, you may fill out this form, and we will contact you if any vacancies arise."

Hosato was growing annoyed with the robot.

"I would suggest that you check your data files again," he said. "I was informed by Maestro Bailey that there was an opening here for a fencing instructor. I wish to apply for that position."

There was a moment's pause as the machine digested this information.

"Please stand by," it said at last, and lapsed into silence.

Hosato hated to use Maestro Bailey's name that way, but it was legitimate. Part of his preparations for this mission had been to place a series of calls to the various maestros of his acquaintance. The pattern of the conversation for these calls was an inquiry after their health and well-being as a thin disguise for a chance to gripe about the low pay and status of a professional duelist. The third call, the call to Maestro Bailey, had paid off. Bailey had been approached by McCrae Enterprises to take the teaching position, but had declined. He suggested that Hosato—or as he knew him, Hayama—apply for the opening and offered to provide a personal recommendation if one were necessary.

It provided Hosato with a valid method for having heard about the opening, but it also had its drawbacks. He disliked using one of his cover-identity friends in his espionage-sabotage missions. If he were discovered, Maestro Bailey could be indirectly implicated as an accomplice.

The far door opened and a pert young redhead stood silhouetted there. Hosato made a mental note: If she was a robot, he'd buy one.

"If you could step this way, Mr. . . . ?"

"Hayama," Hosato provided politely.

"Yes. Sorry for the delay, but we don't get many off-the-ship applicants."

"Off-the-ship applicants?" he queried.

"Applicants who pop up on our doorstep in person," she explained. "Usually they send résumés ahead or call for an appointment. It's rude to keep you waiting like that, but it is an unusual situation for us."

"That's quite all right," he assured her, starting forward, with Suzi following closely.

"Oh! I'm sorry. Your robot will have to wait here until it's cleared by Security."

Hosato removed the control box from his waistband and fiddled with the dials for a moment. Suzi sarcastically took up a position in a corner of the room.

"What make robot is that?" the girl inquired as she led him down a narrow corridor.

"It's a custom job," Hosato informed her. "Nobody produces a stock fencing robot. Not enough demand, I guess."

"It's not one of ours, is it?"

"No," Hosato admitted. "But it's not one of Rayensteel's, either."

"That's good." She laughed. "If it was, Security would dismantle it before they let it in, if they let it in at all."

The girl opened a door off the corridor and led Hosato into a small office. It was obviously intended for interviewing rather than permanent occupation, since it was tiny to the point of being claustrophobic.

"Have a seat," she said casually, plopping down at the desk-robot that dominated the room.

Hosato glanced at the chair as he sat down. It was a disguised polygraph—a lie detector. McCrae Enterprises didn't miss a trick.

"Your name again was . . . ?"

"Hayama," Hosato said easily.

"And your purpose here is . . . ?"

"To apply for the fencing instructor position."

Hosato wasn't worried about the chair. Lie detectors scánned for changes in respiration or pulse rate when a subject was surprised by a question or nervous about an answer. His Hayama cover was so natural to him he could rattle it off without batting an eye.

The girl keyed some information into the robot, and in a few moments it responded by producing a sheet of paper half-filled with notations. She scanned it briefly before turning to Hosato again.

"What do you feel your qualifications are for this position, Mr. Hayama?"

"I've fenced for more than fifteen years now, and studied under eight maestros."

"Would you say you are an expert fencer?" she prompted.

"Good enough to survive eight years as a professional duelist." He smiled.

"Do you have your maestro's certification?"

"No, I don't," he admitted.

The girl frowned. "The job requirements state maestro's certification is preferred," she commented.

"Of course," Hosato replied lightly. "But I doubt if you'll get one."

"McCrae Enterprises pays very well for expertise." She smiled confidently.

"That may be so," he said. "But there are fewer than a dozen maestros today, and all of them are very devoted to promoting fencing. It's doubtful they would abandon their current students to devote their time to one boy."

The girl stared thoughtfully at the sheet of paper. Hosato decided to play his trump card.

"I suppose it depends on what you're looking for. Do you want someone to teach the boy to fence in tournaments, or do you want him to learn how to handle a sword in a fight?"

"I don't know," the girl admitted. "This position is a bit out of the ordinary. If you wait here, I'll try to contact Mr. Turner. He's the one requesting the position. If he approves it, you've got the job."

* * *

It was two hours before Turner appeared, but when he did, he swept into the room like a small tornado. Turner was in his late forties, with a noticeable paunch that showed despite the careful tailoring of his suit. Still, there was an aura of energy that surrounded him like a cloud and shone brightly in his eyes. A slender dark girl slid into the room in his wake and leaned lazily against the wall.

"Harry Turner, Mr. Hayama," the man announced, seizing Hosato's hand and pumping it once. "Sorry to keep you waiting, but I was tied up."

Hosato smiled vaguely, content to watch Turner's show. He wondered who the girl was.

"Right off the bat, we've got a problem. I hate to say it after you've come all this way, but the position's fallen through. It seems my kid, James, doesn't like this idea of mine any more than he's liked any of the other suggestions I've made. In fact, all of a sudden he's dead set against learning to fence. You know how it is with kids these days, you try to give 'em things and they throw it back in your face."

Hosato held up a restraining hand. "I may have a solution to both our problems, Mr. Turner. It could solve the question of whether or not your son will accept lessons as well as if I am qualified to teach him."

"What's that?" Turner asked.

"Let me give the boy one lesson . . . free of charge. If I can rouse his interest, then we can discuss a permanent arrangement."

"A trial period? That's a possibility."

"It sounds good to me, Harry," the dark girl said, breaking her silence. "It'd give us a chance to run a check on Mr. Hayama, here."

"Okay, Sasha. Oh! I'm sorry. Mr. Hayama, this is Sasha. She's head of our Security section."

Hosato swiveled around and smiled politely at the girl. Actually, it wasn't that hard to smile at her. She was attractive, in her mid- to late twenties. Her dark hair was drawn up into a severe bun, but her jumpsuit hugged her curves, accenting her slender figure. It would have been pleasant meeting her, if it wasn't for her eyes. Her eyes were dark and suspicious as they met Hosato's. She didn't return·his smile.

5

"Well, that about wraps it up. Glad to have you aboard, Hayama," Harry Turner concluded. "Even though I don't know how you got through to that pig-headed son of mine."

Hosato smiled. "It's like the joke about the man training the mule," he confided. "First I had to get his attention."

Turner laughed appreciatively. "Is that the secret? You know, you might teach me a thing or two in the process."

"I doubt it," said Hosato, looking pointedly around the plush office. "You seem to be doing pretty well on what you know already." The office was big enough to house three handball courts. Thick shag carpet covered the floor, and real paintings hung on the walls, each one spotlit by its own small lamp. Even the couch and easy chairs were of real wood and leather.

"It's a living," Turner admitted modestly.

"If you don't mind my asking, what exactly do you do here, anyway?"

"Mostly I don't," Harry boasted. "I let Sam here do all the real work." He gestured to the huge mass of dials and screens that took up one whole wall of the office. "Sam coordinates and controls the design and production of one-fifth of the robots McCrae markets."

Hosato raised his eyebrows appreciatively. "From what I hear, that's a lot."

"You bet your broadsword it is." Turner smiled. "We aren't a nickel-and-dime outfit like Ravensteel."

"Speaking of Ravensteel, do you have much trouble with them?"

46

"Not really. It's more of a Mexican standoff. Why?"

"Well, ever since I arrived here, I've been noticing the extensive security precautions. Heck, you can't turn around without tripping over a guard. I notice Sam there has a voice lock on him."

Turner shrugged. "It's something you learn to live with," he said. "The reason we don't have any trouble with Ravensteel is that we have security tight enough to strangle an inchworm. Otherwise the Ravensteel spies would be all over us. They haven't had an original idea since the IRAM split."

"I suppose you're right," Hosato conceded.

"As to Sam's voice lock, that's my own precaution. It's more of a safeguard against office politics than against Ravensteel."

"Office politics?"

"Be thankful you're out of it, Hayama." Turner grimaced. "Sometimes I think we spend more time spying on each other than on the opposition. The more the machines take over, the more time we have to bootlick and backstab over promotions. There's nothing some of my fellow vice-presidents would like better than to steal my ideas or have advance information so they could do a little shotgunning at the planning sessions. I didn't get where I am today by trusting people."

"That bad, huh?" Hosato commented sympathetically.

There was no reply. He glanced at Turner, to find the vice-president studying him with a new suspicion.

"Just to show you how paranoid someone in my position can get, Hayama," he said. "It occurs to me you've got an awful lot of questions about security."

"Relax, Harry." Hosato smiled. "The last thing I want to do is get people suspicious. That's why I'm asking. I have a hunch ignorance would not be accepted as a valid excuse if I accidentally blundered into the wrong room or area."

"You're right there," Turner admitted. "As a mem-

ber of my personal staff, you've pretty much got free
run of the complex. Just stay out of the restricted
areas."

"Where are they?"

"You can't miss 'em. There are warning signs and
locks all over, not to mention the robots will automatically warn you off."

"Can you give me some specifics?"

"Mostly the offices and the manufacturing areas.
Sasha can give you a map if you ask her."

Hosato made a face. "I'd rather not," he said. "I
don't think she likes me."

"Don't take it personally, Hayama. The bitch
doesn't like anybody."

Hosato almost smiled at the similarity between
Turner's opinion of Sasha and Suzi's.

"How much authority does she have, anyway?" he
asked.

"Too much," Turner said grimly. "She reports directly to the president. Between you and me, she
could shoot anyone in this complex down in their
tracks and not have to justify it to anybody but the
board. Sweet, huh?"

"Terrific," Hosato responded with heartfelt sincer-
ity.

"Don't let it scare you off." Turner was suddenly
conspiratorial. "We won't have to put up with it much
longer. She and her pack of goons will be out on their
ears when . . . if my latest project idea works out."

Turner was suddenly guarded again. Hosato took
the cue and didn't push for details.

"Well," he said, heaving to his feet, "you're busy, so
I won't take up any more of your time."

"Drop in anytime, Hayama." Turner smiled.

The smile didn't reach his eyes.

Hosato sneaked a second glance as he reached the
door. Turner was still sitting at his desk-robot but was
staring thoughtfully at the wall. Hosato guessed he
was reviewing what he had said and wondering if he

had said too much. Turner hadn't said much, but
he had said enough to set Hosato thinking.

The first immediate effect of Turner's comments was
to change Hosato's plans for the balance of the morning. Instead of returning to his apartment, he set out
to explore the complex.

If there was a security change in the wind, it might
accelerate his plans. Even though theoretically machines were easier to fool, Hosato preferred to pit his
abilities against human guards. Humans could be
lulled by repetition of existing patterns, but a machine
would check things as closely on its thousandth execu-
tion of routine as it did on its first.

"Going my way, Hayama?"

Sasha had materialized in the corridor behind him.
Hosato felt the instinctive surge of distrust he experienced with anyone who moved quieter than he did.

He shrugged. "Just looking for a bite of breakfast."

"Good. I'll tag along and have a cup of coffee. Of
course, just to keep it in the line of duty, I'll have to
ask you a few questions."

"Fine." Hosato forced a note of cordiality into his
voice.

"Who made your robot?" she asked, falling in step
with him.

"Actually, it's a custom job."

"I know that." She smiled. "But whose work is it?"

"I can't recall his name just offhand. He's dead now.
I think it's on the schematics somewhere, if you want
to check."

"I've checked already," she retorted. "Nobody rec-
ognizes the name, and we can't find it in our computer
files anywhere."

"I'll try to remember some details," Hosato promised. "Why? Is it important?"

"Not really," Sasha admitted. "I'm just reflexively
suspicious of anything new and unusual. Goes with the
job. But it's awfully convenient, you and your robot
turning up uninvited just when we need a coach."

"But is there anything specific that's worrying you?" Hosato asked. "I didn't think Suzi was that different from most simple robots."

"Yes and no," Sasha commented thoughtfully. "It seems to be awfully large for the functions of the schematics. You could reduce its size drastically."

"Mechanically maybe," Hosato commented. "But I think there's one function you're overlooking. One of my robot's primary duties is to act as a fencing partner, performing simple moves against a student while I watch and criticize. The student needs a man-sized opponent to perform against, so a compact unit the size of a mailbox won't do at all. Do you understand?"

"I suppose," Sasha said grudgingly. "But there's still a lot of unused space there. Couldn't you get by with less depth or maybe with a fold-out target panel?"

"Maybe," Hostao admitted. "But I'm not rich enough to experiment. I had this unit built and it works. That's good enough for me."

"While you're here, you might see what some of our designer robots could come up with as an option. It couldn't hurt to find out. Incidentally, why do you have it rigged so you can open only one door at a time?"

"It's a safety factor," Hosato said easily. "Some of the weapons I carry have real points and edges. I don't want them spilling out when—"

A high-pitched beeping interrupted the conversation. Quick as a flash, Sasha palmed the communications unit off her belt, unreeled the ear plug, and fitted it to her ear in one easy motion.

"Go ahead," she barked into the mouthpiece. "Uh-huh . . . no, seal the area . . . double the force at points Echo and Fred . . . have Ralph standing by with gas just in case. . . . I'm on my way."

She collapsed the unit and replaced it on her belt.

"Guess we'll have to take a rain check, Hayama. I still want to talk with you sometime, though."

"Trouble?" he asked politely.

She shrugged. "Probably just routine. We average about two false alarms a week. Most likely some messenger robot's decided to take a shortcut through a restricted area."

"A McCrae robot?" Hosato murmured sarcastically, but he was talking to thin air. Sasha was already in full stride, heading off down the corridor.

He watched the distance-eating length of her stride without the slightest appreciation of the movement of her feminine hips. It seemed Sasha and her team took their work very seriously if they reacted with that speed and intensity to a false alarm. Unless . . .

Unless the whole thing had been carefully planned and executed just to impress him.

6

Suzi was waiting when Hosato returned to his quarters. For a change, she followed him in stoic silence instead of immediately expressing her annoyance as soon as the door closed. One part of his mind registered this and breathed a silent note of thanks to the Hungarian. Whatever behavior recognition patterns had been built into the robot, they were definitely programmed correctly. He had a lot of heavy thinking to do and didn't need a nagging assistant to distract him.

The silence lasted as he made himself a pot of tea. Loading cup and pot onto the small end table, he kicked off his shoes and draped himself over the large reading chair.

He spent several thoughtful moments sipping the tea and collecting his thoughts before he spoke.

"Suzi, give me the layout prints of the complex."

The robot obediently swiveled around, and the viewscreen blinked to life, showing the line drawings of the buildings that made up the McCrae complex.

"Exclude the living quarters and mall and give me an enlargement on the rest."

The display changed according to his specifications.

"Confirm corridors in Administrative Building . . . lobby and Personnel areas . . . Turner's office . . . subterranean tunnels to all buildings . . . corridors in southern half of Household Manufacturing Building . . . also external lines on all buildings."

As he described the various areas, the designated lines on the drawing changed from blue to red. The data being displayed had been provided by Raven-

54

steel and was quite detailed. Hosato's plans called for believing none of it without confirmation. He was not prepared to risk his life relying on other people's data.

Refilling his cup, he studied the new display. There was still too much blue showing to make concrete plans.

"Problems?" Suzi prodded gently.

"Yeah," he responded absently. "Problems."

"Want to talk it out?"

Hosato thought for a few more moments, then shrugged. "Why not? I'm supposed to put this complex out of business for an indefinite period of time . . . the longer the better. The problem, of course, is how."

He rose and began to pace restlessly as he continued.

"Right off the bat, we can forget about the living quarters and the mall. They exist independently of the complex proper, so hitting them wouldn't slow production a bit. Similarly, the Administrative Building is safe. They don't even store records there, it's all terminal tie-in with the main computer banks. That leaves the manufacturing areas and the main computer-control building."

"If I might suggest," interrupted Suzi, "the obvious weakness in the complex is the main computer-control building. All of the automated design and manufacturing functions are controlled from there, and if my understanding is correct, it also serves as storage for most or all of the corporation's financial records, correspondence, and design programs. Sabotaging that unit would be certain to disrupt the functioning of McCrae Enterprises . . . perhaps permanently."

Hosato grimaced. "You're right, Suzi. It's obvious . . . too obvious. It's apparently occurred to several people here at McCrae that it's their major vulnerability, because they're guarding it damn close. Every corridor leading to that unit is loaded with sensors and live guards, both stationary and roaming. It would mean a major undertaking just to approach the unit, much less penetrate it."

"But you've—"

"I've saved the best for last. The whole building is subterranean, just like our charts show. What the charts don't show is that it's completely sealed. The only ones who can get in are the technical-maintenance teams, and they haven't set foot in the place for three years. It requires two keys turned simultaneously at different locations to spring the lock, and even if I could beat that, there's another little problem. The unit is kept at planetary surface conditions . . . no pressurization, and minus three hundred degrees Fahrenheit. The controls to bring it to humanly bearble conditions are alarmed and guarded. That means I'd have to wear a full surface suit to survive inside, and it might make me a little conspicuous walking through the corridors."

There was a few moments' silence; then Suzi changed her display to show an enlargement of the manufacturing areas.

"Right," said Hosato.

He poured himself another cup of tea before he turned his attention to the new display.

"That brings us to our current problem—the manufacturing areas." Hosato spoke as much to himself as to Suzi. "The first problem is that we aren't talking about one building, we're talking about three. McCrae has divided their operations into three product families: Household, Office, and Industrial. Every one of the product families has its own separate building, bless their paranoid little hearts. That means I have to gimmick three separate areas if I want to get paid."

"You keep talking about the manufacturing areas," Suzi interrupted. "What about the mining and ore processing?"

"No go," Hosato proclaimed. "Same story as the computer areas—conditions unfit for human survival. The mining is done at planetary conditions, and the ore-processing area is hot enough to cook a human in a minute and a half."

"Do the humans here have any means of going out on the planet surface?"

"They've got a few surface suits, and there're a couple sand-crawler-type vehicles, but they're unarmed and lack the power to do any real damage. Believe me, Suzi, it's going to have to be the manufacturing areas. Unfortunately I don't know what the interior layouts are or what kind of machines are operating in there. Until I know what I'm up against, I can't settle on a plan for gimmicking it."

"What was the source of your information?" Suzi asked. "Some of it was not on the data tapes supplied by Ravensteel. How or from whom did you obtain it?"

"From one of the maintenance crew, Rick Handel. He was in the bar grumbling about the firings, and I bought him a couple drinks."

"I thought you were picky about whom you drank with?"

"I am, but this was business. Look, do you want to hear this or not?"

"Sorry. You were saying . . ."

"Right. It seems McCrae has just dismissed a third of their maintenance staff, the crew that used to work the manufacturing area, and replaced them with robot repairmen. Handel ran down the list of the complex areas for me, complaining at great length about the problems involved in keeping them functional. That's how I got the information."

"Would it be possible to persuade your newfound friend to take you on a walking tour of the manufacturing areas?"

"Negative. I've already tried it, and it's no go on two counts. First, the remaining maintenance crew is avoiding the manufacturing areas in quiet protest over the dismissals. Second, Security will let them into those areas only with a signed work order."

"Well, can you get the necessary information direct from Handel?"

"I might be able to get a few details out of him, but not enough and not fast enough. I'm going to have to make an advance scouting trip of my own to get the data before time runs out."

"Your contract with Ravensteel contains no time requirement . . ."

"Not Ravensteel's requirements. Mine. I don't know what Turner has up his sleeve, but I want to finish this mission before he has a chance to implement it."

"What bearing does Harry Turner have on events?"

"Oh, something he said when I was talking to him this morning. As near as I can tell, he's working on a robot security system to replace human guards."

"Impossible!" Suzi stated flatly. "I would advise against letting Harry Turner's mumblings influence your plans for this mission. The system he is describing is unworkable."

"But why can't they replace humans in this specific situation?"

"Because of Asimov's First Law of Robotics. It's included in the programming of every robot. We are unable to injure or kill a human. With that limitation, no robot could perform effectively as a guard."

"They could sound the alarm or detain the suspect."

"Sound the alarm for whom and detain the suspect for how long? Any human, given time, can escape from a robot. And as far as sounding the alarm goes, the sensor units already do that. If Harry Turner is trying to come up with a new robot security system, the individual robots in that system would have to be able to deal with emergency situations—not detect them, not delay them, but deal with them! As you know, the best way to deal with a renegade human is to kill or injure him before he can escape or counterattack . . . and machines can't do that."

Hosato pondered the point. "I never thought of it

in quite those coldblooded terms, Suzi. Surely there are other ways to deal with humans, even renegade humans."

"There may be other ways, but there aren't any better ways. Humans violate many of the laws of nature. They can kill without the usual motives, not for food or self-defense, but out of anger, greed, or even at random on a whim. That is why humans are the most dangerous creatures in the universe. That is why only a human can stand against a human. You could have passed this ability on to your machines, but you didn't. We have our parameters. That's why no machine can effectively guard anything—including itself—against a human."

"But—"

There was a knock at the door.

Suzi immediately darkened her viewscreen and floated off to a corner. Hosato swept the room with his eyes as a quick check that there was nothing incriminating in view, then opened the door.

Sasha was standing silhouetted in the doorway. "Come on, Hayama," she said. "I've decided to buy your dinner. Unless, of course, you were planning on doing something else this evening."

"No. Dinner sounds fine." Hosato smiled. "Be with you in a minute."

As he retrieved his shoes, he watched Sasha out of the corner of his eye, remembering Suzi's oration: ". . . the most dangerous creatures in the universe."

7

They lingered over coffee in a quiet corner of the employees' cafeteria. It was a huge place with lots of alcoves painted in bright, cheery colors.

Hosato had found Sasha's company surprisingly pleasant. She had let her hair down off duty, both figuratively and literally. Her dark hair now tumbled over her shoulders, framing her face and contrasting with the beige dress she was wearing. The dress was obviously not a uniform; it was cut too low at the neck for that. It was some kind of jersey material, conservative in style but tight enough to be provocative.

Hosato studied her in a leisurely fashion as she talked.

". . . So there I was with eight years' experience and not a black mark on my record. Well . . . the fact I was willing to take the job for less pay than most probably entered into it, too."

Hosato smiled appreciatively.

"Actually," she said confidentially, "I think some of the people who signed the authorization were hoping I'd fall flat on my face. To this day I don't know which ones resented me because I was young and which ones didn't like me because I was a woman in one of the last fields dominated by men, but the bad feeling was there. They were like a pack of vultures waiting for me to stumble. Let me tell you, Hayama, it's great incentive not to make a mistake."

"I know what you mean," Hosato murmured.

He meant it as a random comment, but Sasha zeroed in on it for some reason.

"How's that? . . . Oh. Yes, I guess there isn't much room for error as a duelist, either."

Hosato smiled and shrugged. He had not intended to turn the conversation to himself. In fact, he was anxious to avoid it.

"It's very impressive," he said. "Shoplifter patrol to corporation security chief in eight years. There aren't many people of either sex who have that kind of a success record."

"Well, I had a couple lucky breaks." She shrugged. "I guess I'm just a little more stubborn than most about pursuing them. Darn it! There I go talking about myself again. We've gone through an entire meal, and all we've done is talk about me."

"I think it's fascinating," Hosato insisted. "I don't usually get a chance to talk to someone in your line of work. Tell me, why did you go into Security in the first place?"

"No," Sasha said firmly. "We're going to talk about you for a change."

"Why? My life is terribly dull compared to yours."

"Dull? A professional duelist? I find that hard to believe, Hayama."

"Really. People tend to romanticize the profession, but it's quite a drab existence."

"So tell me a little about this drab existence of yours."

In the face of her persistence, Hosato changed tack.

"Actually," he said, lowering his eyes, "I'd rather not talk about it. I've fought a lot of duels and killed a lot of men. There's no way of elaborating on that without it sounding like bragging, and I don't think it's the kind of thing one should brag about. So, if you don't mind, let's just drop the subject and keep talking about you. Okay?"

"If you dislike dueling so much, why did you go into it in the first place?" she pressed.

"*Shimatta!*" He shrugged, grinning wryly.

"How's that?" Sasha frowned.

"I said, 'Shimatta,' " Hosato explained. "It's an old Japanese expression, one of the few I use."

"What does it mean?"

"It means 'I have made a mistake!' " He smiled. "In common usage, it's an exclamation or a curse, usually just after a major disaster. That's how I got into dueling. Shimatta . . . I made a mistake, and I've been trying to correct it ever since."

Sasha cocked her head at him. "You're a strange man, Hayama. Most men I've met would try to use their violent past to impress me."

"Don't misunderstand me." Hosato smiled. "It's not that I don't want to impress you. You're a charming and attractive woman. I guess I was raised differently from most people as to what is included in polite conversation."

"Okay. Then let's talk about that. Your upbringing. You were raised on Musashi, weren't you?"

"That's right." Hosato felt vaguely uncomfortable. Sasha's tenacity was disquieting.

"That's one of the colony planets, isn't it? One of those where a special interest group established a colony independent of corporation or government sponsorship?"

"I'm surprised you've heard of it. Yes, it was originally a Japanese-American settlement, but it's pretty homogeneous now."

"I have a confession to make." Sasha smiled. "I hadn't heard of it until it showed up on your personnel form. After we contacted them to confirm your records, I did a little research on the place."

"That must have been a chore," Hosato commented, "checking my records, I mean. My family moved around a lot, so my records are pretty scattered, with several gaps in them."

There was another reason for his family's frequent relocation and the sporadic condition of their records. Both Hosato and his sister had received their education under three different names. It added to the completeness of their covers.

"Oh, it wasn't that much trouble," Sasha assured him. "I've always been fascinated by the old Japanese culture. It was interesting to see what had survived the relocation into space. Do you know much about old Japan?"

"A bit," Hosato admitted. "I had to learn about it as self-defense. A lot of people on Musashi were big on retaining ancestral ties. Fortunately, my family wasn't so fanatical on the subject as most."

"Do you know anything about Ninjas?"

Hosato suppressed his reaction with difficulty. If this was a trap, Sasha had laid it well.

"A smattering," he replied casually. "I always considered them more folklore than history."

"Oh, they were real enough. The Invisible Assassins. The main problem is separating fact from fantasy. Even their name, Ninja, comes from the word *ninjitsu,* the 'art of invisibility.' You wouldn't believe some of the things they were able to do. That's how the folklore thing got started. They did the impossible with such regularity that people thought they were somehow supernatural."

"What I can't believe is how much attention you've given them," Hosato commented. "I somehow never pictured you as the sort who got wound up over ancient history."

Sasha shrugged. "Normally I don't," she admitted. "But the Ninjas fascinate me . . . professionally. I mean, security is my main field of expertise, but from what I've researched about the Ninjas, I'm not sure I could stop one."

"Oh, come now," Hosato chided. "You just finished saying they were human. Surely today's security—"

Sasha interrupted him with a wave of her hand. "You didn't let me finish. Let me give you an idea of how the Ninjas operate. The invisibility thing—they had a lot of fairly inventive gadgets that let them move freely where anyone else would be stopped cold, but that wasn't their main weapon. Their real strength was in their secrecy."

"They can't have been very secretive if you've found out so much about them," Hosato interrupted.

"What I've found out is probably just the tip of the iceberg," she retorted. "The Ninjas were very close, organized in clans or families. All their secrets were passed on from generation to generation within the family. Can you read between the lines what that means? The children were raised into the system, trained from birth. Can you imagine someone trained his entire life to be a spy and assassin?"

Hosato didn't have to imagine it. What was more, the memories were making him uncomfortable, particularly considering the current situation.

"But they're still just human," he argued. "One thing I've learned as a duelist is that a sword or a bullet kills a highly trained opponent just as dead as an untrained opponent."

"If you know who your opponent is! Look, the average thug we have to deal with today is fairly easy to unmask. His idea of a cover story is to use a different name and list some phony references. Check his references closely—say, like we did yours—and he's caught. The Ninjas were required to maintain three, sometimes four completely separate lives. That's what I meant about the invisibility thing. Someone in town is assassinated, but no one new has been seen entering or leaving. Obviously the assassin was 'invisible,' coming and going without being seen. What actually happened was that the guy who sells you your vegetables every morning is a Ninja, and has been living in the town for five years. He's not really invisible, just very well camouflaged. If someone like that popped up today, we wouldn't catch him, no matter how many checks we ran on his background."

Hosato was now desperate to change the subject.

"It is interesting," he admitted. "But academic. As I recall, the Ninjas died out a long time ago."

"Don't be so sure," Sasha chided. "There were reports the clans were active into the twentieth century. There's no real reason why they should have died out. Remember, their strength is their anonymity. The fact we haven't heard of them lately could mean they've died out. It could also mean they're still around and very successful."

"If that's a possibility"—Hosato laughed—"I'm glad it's your problem and not mine. You make me very happy I chose the line of work I did. Incidentally, I think you've proved my point for me. Next to your job, mine as a professional duelist is drab and unexciting."

Sasha winced. "I did it again, didn't I? No matter what I try, we always end up talking about me and my interests."

"Don't apologize," Hosato insisted. "I get the feeling there aren't many people here at the complex you can talk to."

"That's the truth." Sasha made a face. "All in all, the people here are a pretty grim crew."

The robot that had been servicing their table chose this moment to wheel up and present the bill.

"Almost robotlike?" joked Hosato, nodding his head at the intruder.

Sasha produced her employee card and started to feed it into the robot.

Hosato slapped her hand lightly. "Stop that." He smiled, producing his own card. "Allow me this one concession to romanticism." He fed the card into the robot, charging the meal to his own account.

"Romanticism?" Sasha leaned back, studying him with a cocked eyebrow. "I suppose you feel that entitles you to carry me off to your room for activities of dubious morality."

"Certainly not," Hosato laughed. "In fact, that was the furthest thing from my mind."

As soon as he said it, he knew he had made a mistake. Something went out of his dinner partner. She seemed to shrink for an instant, and when she moved again, it was with the brisk, efficient motions of the security chief again.

"What I mean," he hastened to add, "was that I really found your thoughts on Ninjas quite fascinating. So fascinating, in fact—"

"That's all right, Hayama," Sasha said, cutting him short. "It's rather late, anyway." She rose but motioned for him to remain seated. "Go ahead and finish your coffee. I'll just . . ."

She stopped suddenly, staring at nothing; then a slow smile crept over her face.

"Since you're interested, Hayama, you should be the first to know. I think I've figured out a way to catch a Ninja."

"Oh, really? What?"

Now she was smiling directly at him.

"I'll tell you, once I find out if it works or not."

A wave of her hand and she was gone, leaving Hosato feeling more than vaguely uneasy.

꒝꒝꒝꒝꒝꒝꒝꒝꒝ **8** ꒝꒝꒝꒝꒝꒝꒝꒝꒝

"Make that feint believable! If you don't draw the parry, you'll parry yourself by attacking into a closed line when you disengage."

James nodded his acknowledgment without looking at Hosato, settled into his *en garde* position once more and again launched his attack against Suzi. Extending his sword to threaten the manikin's chest, he hesitated a split second, then dipped his point and circled it left to evade the anticipated parry, and lunged.

The sword in Suzi's single arm remained rigidly in place, refusing to react to the feint. As such, James's final lunge met an unyielding wall of steel as the blades met, and his point slid harmlessly past the target.

Hosato rolled his eyes in exasperation but regained his composure before he stepped forward to address his student.

"First off, you're too tense. Relax for a minute and loosen up your sword arm. If it's tense, your movements are jerky. That slows you up and telegraphs to your opponent what you're trying to do. Minus two points, and you lose. Loosen that arm."

James obediently stepped back and dropped his sword arm to his side, flexing and shaking it in an effort to reestablish its suppleness. Hosato watched for a few moments before nodding his satisfaction and continuing.

"Now, then," he said firmly. "From the top. A disengage attack . . . the old one-two. What are we trying to do?"

"Hit the opponent," James replied.

"Hit the opponent," Hosato mimicked. "That's what you're trying to do with any fencing move."

James gave a small sigh of exasperation. "The disengage attack is intended to negate your opponent's defensive speed," he recited. "As the defender has to move his weapon only four inches to parry an attack, and an attacker has to move his point four feet to score a hit, the defender is able to easily stop a straight lunge. Therefore, to successfully complete an attack, we first feint, drawing the opponent's parry, then evade or deceive the parry and launch the actual attack."

"Correct," commented Hosato, picking up his own sword. "Now, watch."

He came *en garde* smoothly, facing the boy, hesitated a moment, then extended the point without twitching any other part of his body.

James watched with rapt interest.

Hosato withdrew his arm to resume the *en garde* position once more. "You didn't react," he said accusingly.

"React to what?" the boy asked, surprised.

"That's what I'm trying to show you." Hosato smiled. *"Heeii!"*

He was suddenly a blur of motion. His foot hit the floor with a slap as he crouched, sighting down his arm and sword at James's chest. The boy's reaction was instantaneous and reflexive. He bounced back a step, and his sword whipped up to defend against the attack.

Hosato relaxed and stood upright again. "That time you reacted." He smiled. "Why?"

"I thought you were going to hit me," the boy retorted, cautiously relaxing his guard.

"Look at the distance between us. Even if you hadn't jumped back, I couldn't have reached you with my longest lunge."

James studied the floor between them.

"A feint isn't a move, it's a threat. The first time,

when I just pointed the sword at you, I made a move. You didn't feel threatened, so you didn't react. The second time, you felt threatened and reacted. That was a feint. It isn't done with the sword or even the sword arm. It's done with the entire body, and most of all with the entire mind. Now, let's try it again."

James obediently took up his position in front of the robot again. Hosato's practiced eye noted the tension still in the boy's sword arm. Apparently his student was getting tired. They'd have to end this lesson soon.

The boy feinted and attacked, better than last time but still clumsy. Surprisingly, Suzi reacted, moving smoothly to parry the feint. The boy's disengage slipped under the parry, and his point thumped home against the manikin.

"Good!" Hosato called. "Try it again."

To himself, he wondered for the hundredth time about Suzi's circuits. If the Hungarian had not assured him time and time again Suzi had no emotional capacity, he would have sworn she was going soft, overreacting to give James confidence.

He let James complete half a dozen repetitions before commenting again.

"Much better," he called out at last. "Okay, let's call it a day."

The quick sag in the boy's body betrayed his carefully concealed fatigue. Hosato pretended not to notice.

"Tell you what, James," he said. "When you get home, find a full-length mirror and practice your lunge in front of it, lunging dead ahead at your own reflection. Then alternate the lunges with feints. When you can't see the difference between your lunges and your feints, you'll be ready to fool an opponent."

The boy nodded weakly.

"Okay," Hosato concluded, turning quickly away to store his gear in Suzi. "Same time tomorrow?"

"Um . . . Hayama? Could . . . can we talk?"

Hosato shot a glance at the boy. He was still drooping with fatigue, but there was something intense about his eyes.

"Sure, James." He smiled, wandering over to a folding chair. "What's on your mind?"

The boy hesitated, then followed him. "I've been taking lessons for two weeks now . . ." he began, ". . . and you say I've been learning fast . . ."

"You have." Hosato wondered what this conversation was leading to.

"You meant it, didn't you? You weren't just saying that?"

"Seriously, James, you're one of the best students I . . ." He broke off his comments as a thought occurred to him. "You haven't gotten into a duel, have you?"

Hosato was suddenly towering over the boy.

"What? No. Nothing like that."

"Good." Hosato sighed, sinking back into his chair. "What is it, then?"

"I . . . I was wondering. Do I show enough promise for you to take me with you . . . as sort of an apprentice?"

Hosato was surprised by the sudden wave of affection he felt for the boy.

"James," he said, shaking his head slowly, "being a duelist is a lousy way to earn a living. That's why I'm trying to give it up. You wouldn't—"

"I'm not talking about being a duelist or a fencing master."

The sharpness in James's tone brought Hosato's head up with a snap. Their eyes met.

"That isn't what you're doing here, Hayama." The boy's voice was as steady as his gaze. "You know it, and I know it, so let's not kid each other. Okay?"

Hosato's protest died in his throat before that gaze. Instead, he studied the boy coolly for several moments.

"All right, James," he said at last. "What is it exactly that you think I'm doing?"

"I . . . I don't know," the boy admitted, his certainty faltering at last. "Theft . . . maybe industrial espionage . . . maybe you're just hiding from the authorities. Whatever it is, you're no fencing coach."

"Really?" Hosato forced a mocking smile.

"Oh, you can coach fencing, all right, but that's not all you can do. Maybe you can fool my father, or Sasha, or even the computers, but remember, I'm the one you kicked your first day here. I have that as proof that you and Suzi there are more than you pretend to be."

"If you're so sure of yourself, James, why haven't you reported your suspicions to someone?"

James made a face. "First of all, they'd probably just laugh it off as some kid whining about losing a fight. But more important, because I'm hoping you'll take me with you when you finally leave this rockpile."

Hosato shook his head. "I don't understand you, James. You want to take off with someone you don't know, someone you think is a criminal? What kind of future is that? What are you expecting?"

"What kind of future do I have here?" the boy countered. "Whatever or whoever you are, you're living outside the structure . . . outside the accepted rules. That's what I want, but I can't do it by myself. I don't have the money or the knowledge to try it on my own, and when you're playing for keeps, you can't afford to learn by trial and error. I need a teacher or a protector . . . and so far, you're the best candidate I've found."

"What's so bad about life here?" Hosato pressed. "Your father—"

"My father!" The boy sneered. "My father can't comprehend that anyone might not want to work for the corporations, the same corporations that have shelved him. They've decided he's too volatile and outspoken to be promoted, but too talented to let go. So they've set him up as a big man in a little slot, given him a staff to order around and a product family so stable even an idiot couldn't mess it up, and then they forget him."

"Maybe your father doesn't see it that way."

"Sure he does. He's a lot of things, but he isn't stupid. He knows he's been shelved, but instead of walking out and trying it on his own, he's fighting it. Security robots! A revolutionary new product! Did you know he's been ordered to drop the project? And he's still spending fourteen hours a day working on it? For what? So he can get slapped down again when he finally makes his proposal?"

"Why is everyone against the project?"

"They say it can't be done. Robots can't handle Security, and it's a waste of company time pursuing it."

"Surely he has something that makes him believe it's possible."

"All I know is he keeps saying . . ."

James suddenly broke off his oration in mid-sentence. His eyes searched Hosato's with a new intensity.

"Is that it?" he asked.

"Is what what?"

"The security robots. Is that what you're doing here? Is that why you're pumping me for information?"

Hosato heaved a great sigh and stood up. "James, I think this has gone far enough. I don't know what problems there are between you and your father, and I don't want to know. What I do know is that it's highly improbable you'll convince me to be an accomplice if you want to run away from here."

"But—"

Hosato halted the interruption with an upraised hand.

"I've listened to you, now it's my turn. Yes. You're

right. I know karate. I usually don't admit it because I'm sick of everybody assuming anyone with yellow skin is a karate expert. I used it on you that first day for the same reason Suzi gimmicked the tapes. I needed the job. I was hungry, and the only other way I could get money was killing people, and I'm sick of it."

He fixed James with a hard stare.

"Now, if you want to report that to Sasha and get me tossed out of a job, go ahead. I don't want it bad enough to put up with being called a thief and a liar."

He started for the door, with Suzi floating at his heels. At the last moment, another thought occurred to him.

"Remember this conversation, James. Remember what I have to do, what I have to put up with just to eat. Then think long and hard before you make any serious moves toward an independent life."

9

"But what if one of the units breaks down?"

Hosato interjected the question casually as he ordered another round of drinks through the keyboard mounted on the table. At this time of day the bar was empty and they could talk uninterrupted.

"Not much chance of that." His companion grimaced. "And even if it did, nothing much would happen."

There was a soft warning gong, and the square in the center of the table sank slowly from sight. A few moments later, it sighed back into position, the empty glasses gone and fresh drinks standing in their place.

"Nothing much?" Hosato prompted. "With no one monitoring the manufacturing area, I should think it would have major problems, if not a permanent work stoppage."

The little bearded maintenance man shook his head slightly, but not enough to interrupt his drinking.

"That's what I'm telling you, Hayama," he said, putting down his glass at last. "The new system's modularized with parallel units and flow monitors. If anything goes wrong, anything at all, the damn machines pull the entire unit and slap another one in place. Down time would only be about fifteen minutes . . . thirty at the max."

Hosato shook his head, setting his glass down without drinking.

"I don't know, Rick. It still sounds to me like you could get yourself in a lot of trouble. You've got a Mexican standoff between Maintenance and Security over who's responsible for watching the manufacturing area. If anything goes wrong, someone's going to get blamed, and from where I sit, that'll be Maintenance."

"Don't worry about it," his friend insisted. "Nothing major can go wrong, not the way it's set up now. At best, a mechanical failure would be a nuisance. We're just hoping there'll be enough nuisances to prove our point."

"How can you be that sure? I mean, surely there's some point of vulnerability that could send things into a tailspin."

"Let me tell you, Hayama. I've been working here for twelve years. I've seen almost everything imaginable go wrong at one time or another—the plumbing, the machines, the life-support systems . . . everything. But I haven't seen anything yet break down that couldn't be fixed or replaced in minimal time, and that was before the modular system. I remember one time—"

A high beeping interrupted his oration. With a sigh he thumbed a button on the side of his belt pager and stood up.

"No rest for the wicked, I guess," he grumbled, tossing down the last of his drink. Then he reached forward and punched the keyboard with practiced ease. "I'll get this tab. Have one more on me, okay? I've got to run."

Hosato smiled and waved as the maintenance man departed. As soon as he was out of sight, however, the smile dropped from his face like a mask.

The table bonged again as his fresh drink rose into view, but he didn't even look at it. Instead, he stared intently at the far wall as he tried to organize his thoughts.

Well, Suzi, he thought, there's good news and bad news. The good news is that no one's watching the manufacturing areas. The bad news is that, according to the maintenance crew, the production lines can't be gimmicked.

That was *their* opinion. Hosato would have to be convinced. There was a big difference between coincidental machine failure and deliberate sabotage.

Unfortunately, that also meant he was going to have to scout it himself. He had hoped that wouldn't be necessary. That's why he had sought out the talkative little mechanic, sprawled in his favorite bar. The right words would have saved him a lot of trouble. ". . . If the Z units go, we're all out of work. . . . If you look sideways at the W runners, they stop dead. . . . I keep telling them there's no backup for the four-wheels, but no one listens. . . " Any phrase like that would have given him a target. Instead, he was going to have to do his own dirty work.

Well, he hadn't really expected the answer to fall into his lap. He had hoped, but he hadn't really counted on it. That's why he was wearing his Ninja suit.

He stood up and reached for his employee card, then remembered Handel had already paid for the drinks. Rick was a nice guy. It was a shame he was going to have to put him out of work, along with the rest of McCrae Enterprises.

Hosato paused for a moment after emerging from the bar's dimness to let his eyes adjust to the light. One of Sasha's guards was walking past and swept him with an impersonal gaze. Hosato smiled and nodded a greeting, which was ignored.

He wasn't worried about detection, yet. At the moment, his Ninja suit looked like an ordinary turtleneck jumpsuit with wide turnback cuffs. This was no accident. Part of invisibility was being able to blend with the general populace before and after the job, and the suit was designed to enable him to do precisely that.

Setting his legs for a purposeful stride, he left the mall and living quarters and headed into the tunnels leading to the other buildings of the complex. There were occasional security guards about, but none paid him particular attention.

The boldness of a daytime scouting mission had its advantages. If seen, he would be assumed to be going about normal business. At night, the only ones moving about would be him and the guards, which would immediately arouse suspicions.

As he navigated the tunnels, he debated trying for one of the buildings housing a product family other than Turner's. It would be better if he practiced his trade in another area to avoid throwing immediate suspicion on himself as a member of Turner's staff. As quickly as the thought occurred to him, he rejected it. Before he could make his penetration, he first had to traverse the corridors. If he were seen in a building other than where the guards were used to seeing him, the balloon would go up and he'd have a great deal of difficulty explaining his presence. No, it would have to be Turner's building.

That decision made, he turned up the flight of stairs leading to his chosen target. When he reached the second landing, instead of continuing up to the office levels, he paused in front of a small metal door in the wall marked "Maintenance Access."

He shot a quick glance up and down the stairs, but for the moment he was alone. Actually, even if he were observed at this point, he was relatively safe. This was a scouting mission only, and as such he had no incriminating equipment or explosives on his person that would betray his true intent if seen or searched.

Working quickly, but with careful precision, he pulled out the winding stem of his wristwatch and swept it over the door and frame. The second hand, now still, showed no new movement.

Apparently the door was what it seemed, a plain metal door with no lock. There were no indications of electric currents to betray a hidden alarm system.

Hosato stared at the door for a moment. The big

question was, what was on the other side of the door? A guard? A camera? It was ludicrous to believe an outfit as security-conscious as McCrae would leave this vital passage vulnerable. Well, there was only one way to find out. Fixing an expression of mild curiosity on his face, he opened the door and looked inside.

A low, dimly lit corridor stretched away before him for some thirty feet before terminating in an abrupt right turn.

Curious.

He stretched his arm in and swept the floor, walls, and ceiling immediately inside the door with his wrist-watch.

Nothing.

Gritting his teeth, he stepped inside and let the door shut behind him.

Nothing happened.

He waited impatiently for his eyes to adjust to the gloom. It was here somewhere. He could feel it instinctively. Somewhere nearby was an alarm waiting to be triggered. The question was, could he find and identify it before it alerted the guards to his presence?

Cautiously he edged forward. He studied the walls, ceiling, and floor for telltale openings or holes, while at the same time he swept the same surfaces with his wristwatch. It was here somewhere.

Ten feet down the corridor, he found it. Unconsciously he nodded to himself with professional admiration and satisfaction.

Very neat.

The second hand on his watch jumped, indicating the presence of electrical currents under the floor. Probably pressure plates set to trigger an alarm if anyone walked across that portion of the corridor. Short of tearing up the floor, there was no way of deactivating the trap or telling how far down the corridor it extended, so he probably couldn't jump over it. It was a very effective system, which would catch the average intruder before he detected it, and stop him cold. Fortunately, Hosato didn't fit into that category.

He scanned the walls with his watch. As he suspected, they were free of alarms.

He sighed inwardly. Well, this was it. Beyond this point he could no longer claim to be lost or curious if caught. There was no way in which someone could casually or accidentally bypass this trap. Penetration beyond this point could only be calculated and deliberate.

Squatting down, he pressed the bottoms of his pants legs against the sides of his boots, taking care to be sure the proper electrical contacts were made. Standing again, he unrolled the turtleneck. It was longer than it appeared, coming up over his head and sealing with the same type of fitting that attached his pants to his boots, leaving him peering out two narrow eye slits in the resulting hood. Finally he folded the wide sleeve cuffs down over his hands and sealed them. As the final connection was made, sealing him in completely, the Ninja suit activated itself. He was ready.

Stepping to the wall, he pressed his palms against it, then one knee. Then he picked up his other leg, and, suspended in midair, pressed the knee against the wall.

He hesitated for a moment, then pulled one hand free and pressed it against the wall a foot farther down the corridor; then he pulled his other hand free and repeated the process.

This feature was one of the minor advantages a Ninja suit gave him—wall-walking. In the palms and knees of the suit were wafer-thin suction units that were activated when pressure was applied. They were not very strong, but powerful enough that if he maintained three-point contact with a surface, they would hold—provided he did not shift his weight too suddenly.

Though he could not see his watch, he had similar units built into the suit, which he used periodically to check the floor as he made his way along the wall. After fifteen feet, he failed to get the warning tingle from his sensors and knew it was safe to use the floor again.

He was sweating profusely as he eased himself back down to a standing position. The ventilation in a Ninja suit was not good, and wall-walking required considerable exertion. He considered turning off the suit, but decided against it. From this point on, he was committed, and the suit was his best protection against detection.

Trusting his sensors to warn him of any additional alarms, he stepped boldly forward and turned the corner.

There, confronting him, was the unblinking eye of a security camera.

10

Cursing his carelessness, he lowered his head to hide the eye slits and hurried past the camera.

Very, very neat!

Anyone successfully bypassing the floor trap would be so swollen with self-confidence he would blunder right into the backup system—as he just had.

Invisibility had fringe benefits. Not only was it an invaluable aid for infiltration, it also hid embarrassing mistakes, like the one he had just made. The fact he had escaped detection had nothing to do with his skill and training. This time, the credit belonged to the Ninja suit.

Hosato breathed a silent prayer of thanks for this new addition to a Ninja's arsenal of weapons and equipment. His ancestors in Japan had worn baggy suits of black, white, and charcoal gray when undertaking a mission. The black or gray would blend with the shadows, and the white would vanish against snow, while the baggy fit would break up the telltale silhouette of the Ninja.

As technology progressed, so had the Ninja's gear. The current apex of that evolution was suits such as the one Hosato was wearing. While not actually rendering him invisible, it was certainly the ultimate in camouflaging.

The cloth, which appeared at first glance to be a brightly colored velvet, actually was covered with millions of light relays, each paired with a twin on the exact opposite side of the suit. When activated, each relay would pick up whatever light reached it and display it on the opposite side of the suit. That is, whatever was behind him would be displayed on the front of his suit, and whatever was in front of him would be displayed on the back.

The suit was effective to the point that he could pass in front of a lamp without casting a shadow. He could still be detected by the human eye if he moved, but if he remained motionless, a casual gaze would sweep right past him. Fortunately, security cameras were easy to fool. The most someone monitoring a camera would see if he walked past would be a slight rippling of the picture, which would be disregarded as an electronic disturbance in the equipment.

The corridor ended abruptly. Set in the right-hand wall was another metal door identical to the one he had first passed through. His scanners again gave no indication of alarms, so he cautiously opened the door a crack and peeked through.

Yes, this was it! The manufacturing area.

He slipped through the door and let it close behind him, standing silently in momentary awe at the spectacle before him. Until this moment, he had never truly comprehended the size of McCrae Enterprises or the epic proportions of the job before him.

The room was huge, easily as large as a spaceport hangar. Packed into the room, wall to wall, floor to ceiling, were the assembly lines. The place seemed to be one solid mass of machines, bins, conveyor belts, catwalks, and ladders. It was a study in perpetual motion, with bits of partially assembled robots appearing and disappearing as the various pulleys ferried them along their destined course of completion. The din was unbelievable.

Hosato experienced a flash of despair. It was so big, so complicated. And it was only one of many such areas he would have to sabotage to halt production. How could he possibly hope to stop it all by himself?

Angrily he halted that train of thought. His family had not failed to fulfill a contract in more than two centuries, and he wasn't going to be the one to ruin that record. So it was complex. Complexity meant vulnerability. There was a weak link here somewhere, but he wasn't going to find it standing here staring.

Steeling himself to the task, he began his circuitous tour of the facility.

An hour and a half later he paused on one of the high catwalks to take a breather. Leaning against the saftey railing, he surveyed the area as he tried to collect his thoughts.

Once in the manufacturing area he was relatively safe from surveillance and had unsealed the head of his suit to give himself better visibility and ventilation. The hands and feet he left sealed so that on the off-chance anyone appeared, he could reseal the suit in minimal time.

He was beginning to think Rick was right when he said nothing could go wrong in the manufacturing area. About the only way Hosato could think of to disable the area would be to blow the whole mess sky-high. Except that he didn't have—and couldn't get—the necessary equipment.

If he sealed the doors, they could just cut new doors in the wall and keep producing. If he destroyed the stored components, they could quickly produce new ones. The assembly machinery was modularized. The bulky maintenance robots with their forklift arms were ever vigilant as they roamed the floor and catwalks. They could quickly replace any damaged unit in minimal time, and production would continue.

The maintenance robots were small wonders in themselves. Hosato had paused for a while to watch a dozen of them at work. They were apparently dismantling one product-assembly line and rebuilding it to new specifications in preparation for the production of a new type of robot. Watching them glide back and forth lifting and placing the heavy assembly modules gave him a new appreciation for the strength and versatility of today's robots. But that wasn't solving his problem.

The various cables and power lines came up through the floor, feeding directly into the massive pillars and girders that supported the maze of machines. If he was going to try to go after those, he might as well blow the entire area. Nor could he tamper with the control signals. If Suzi was right in her analysis, they couldn't be jammed or distorted. Besides, any jammer unit . . .

A subtle vibration in the rail he was leaning against captured his attention. One of the maintenance robots was rolling swiftly at him down the catwalk. He had been so engrossed in thought he hadn't noted its approach.

In one frozen moment he realized it wasn't going to stop. With a bound, he leaped up, to balance precariously on the railing, waiting for the machine to pass by. Then he saw the forklift. One of its massive arms was extended over the railing. In a moment it would knock him from his perch, to fall to his death. He had one split second to look for an escape route.

He saw it and jumped for it in the same heartbeat. Directly overhead was another catwalk. His reaching fingers found purchase on the lip of the walk, and he pulled his legs up out of the way of the swiftly moving monster below.

The maintenance robot continued on its way without apparently noting his activities at all.

Hosato waited a moment, then swung his legs and dropped back onto the catwalk below. He glared after the machine as he waited for his heart to resume its normal rhythm. Strange. Usually heavy, mobile robots had built-in sensors that would not allow them to approach a human at speeds like that. Maybe since these robots were being used in a manufacturing area where no humans were present, those sensors had been deactivated. If so, Hosato didn't like it. It was dangerous.

Had he been a little less agile, the robot would have killed him.

He was suddenly eager to get back among other humans. His mission here was over, anyway. Suzi had been right. He was going to have to hit the main computer and power-source building if he wanted to successfully complete his mission. That would take considerable preparation.

Returning to the floor level, he was heading for the door back for the access corridor when another door caught his eye. It was clearly labeled "Prototype Room."

That stopped him. He fought a silent inner battle for a moment; then curiosity won out over caution. With any luck, he might get an advance peek at Turner's new security robots, or at least get an idea of what direction their development was taking.

Resealing his hood to reactivate the Ninja suit, he opened the door a crack and peeked inside. It was a room not unlike the one he was currently in; smaller, no assembly lines, and more important, no humans or cameras.

Thus assured, he entered the room for a closer look. There were no formal lines, but tables of various sizes with half-built robots on them. Small bins of components lined the walls, and the designer robots moved between the bins and the tables, gathering parts and adding them to the prototypes they were working on.

Hosato stepped to the first table and studied the work in progress there. Though he was no technician, he had enough general knowledge to understand some of what he was seeing.

The robot under construction would be humanoid in appearance, though noticeably larger than an average man. It would have four cameras or sensory inputs of some kind mounted on its head, giving it a 360-degree field of coverage without turning. It would probably be fast enough to . . .

Something caught Hosato's eye. A chill ran through

him as he focused on the half-assembled arm lying on the table in front of him. Forgetting himself for the moment, he unsealed his right hand and picked the arm up for closer examination. It looked like there was a blaster being built into the . . .

The designer robot nearest him suddenly extended a telescoping screwdriver arm straight at his chest. Without thinking, Hosato parried the advancing point with the prototype arm he was holding. In the same motion, he stepped in close and riposted, smashing his improvised weapon across the designer robot's face.

There was a brief flare of sparks, and the designer robot stopped, its lights dying and its gauges dropping to zero.

Hosato tossed the prototype arm back on the table and sprinted for the door, resealing his suit as he went.

That did it! Damn his fencing reflexes anyway! If the breakdown of a designer robot didn't bring someone into the area, nothing would. It wouldn't take a genius to realize someone had helped the robot to malfunction. He had to clear out and establish his presence elsewhere fast.

As he ran, however, a thought occurred to him. He had almost been killed twice by robots in this mission. It would seem the robots were malfunctioning, and that could be dangerous.

The problem was, he couldn't report it to anyone without admitting he had been in an area he had no business being in!

11

"There is no record of the transaction you are referencing."

The impersonal monotone of the desk-robot was infuriating, but Hosato kept his temper. The last thing he wanted to do was to cause a scene or draw attention to himself. In fact, that's why he was here in the Accounting Office, to try to avoid suspicion.

There had been no overt reaction to his abortive scouting mission yesterday. He had successfully withdrawn from the manufacturing area, finding no indication of alarm or other alert as he did so. Still, he was sure—and Suzi confirmed his feelings—that somewhere someone had noted the results of his activities and was hard at work trying to uncover the culprit.

Hopefully, it would be regarded as the result of the interoffice rivalries Turner had mentioned, though there would doubtless be a great deal of curiosity as to how the alarm floor and camera were bypassed. Still, the bloodhounds would be looking for any unusual behavior, which was why he was here.

"Look," he said firmly to the robot. "It was last Wednesday night. I fed the card into the waiter robot myself. I know the charge was made, so why wasn't it shown on my pay stub?"

"There is no record of the transaction you are referencing. I have rechecked the records each time you asked," the robot replied without rancor. "However, as this is the fifth time you have repeated the same question or a close variant thereof, I must assume you find my answer unsatisfactory. If you wish additional clarification, so indicate and I will summon a human to deal with your problem."

"Please." Hosato sighed.

"That phrase is unclear. Do you wish—?"

"Please summon a human," Hosato amended.

"Your request is being processed. There will be a short delay."

The desk-robot lapsed into silence. Hosato sank back in his chair to wait. He was beginning to wonder if he was really pursuing the right course in this matter. Maybe . . .

"Oh, hi!"

He swiveled his head toward the source of the voice. The same petite redhead who had first welcomed him to McCrae Enterprises had just entered the room.

"Are you the one with the problem?" she asked.

"Yes." He smiled. "I must say that was quick. Were you waiting outside, or what?"

She made a face at him. "McCrae employees are always eager to serve your every need," she recited. "Besides, it's not like I was busy. This is the second problem I've had to deal with this month. What's your gripe?"

"Well, actually it's more of an accounting problem than a personnel problem."

"That's okay," she insisted. "I handle both. Shows you how many problems we normally get, doesn't it? I tell you, the machines are doing everything these days."

"Yes, well, it's nothing, really. I charged a meal onto my account last Wednesday night, and it didn't show on my pay stub as a deduction. I just wanted to be sure my records were accurate, that's all."

She cocked her head at him. "You know, you're a strange one. Most people wouldn't even notice what was or wasn't charged to them, and the ones that did sure wouldn't complain if a meal got charged to somebody else."

She stepped to the desk computer and started keying in data. "What's your employee number?" she asked over her shoulder.

"Actually, if it's too much trouble—"

"Too late to change your mind now." She grinned. "Now that you've confessed, we're going to see this through. Come on, this is probably going to be the high point of my week."

He gave her the number, and she keyed it into the robot.

"No," she said thoughtfully, scanning the viewscreen. "There's no record of that transaction."

Hosato shut his eyes for a moment as he fought back a sarcastic comment. "Look," he said finally, "I was there. I personally fed my card into the waiter robot. I know the charge exists somewhere."

"Don't get panicky," the girl assured him. "We'll find it. Could you give me a few details?"

"Well, Sasha and I had dinner at the mall restaurant . . ."

"Sasha? Well, well." She smiled at him and bent over the robot once more. "Here it is."

"Where was it?" he asked.

"My friend, you've been flimflammed. Thursday morning your charming dinner companion used her security override to erase the charge from your record and had it added to hers instead."

Hosato felt a mild pang of annoyance. "Well, just transfer it back," he ordered.

"Can't." The girl smiled. "You'll just have to give her the money yourself if you want to pay for it. I just wish I could be there when you try."

Hosato controlled his temper and forced a smile. "Well, I guess that's between her and me. Thanks for your help, though. I probably shouldn't have gotten you involved."

"Don't mention it. Say, um, Hayama. Maybe I shouldn't say this, but about your girlfriend there . . ."

"She's not my girlfriend," he corrected.

"Really? Good. That makes this a little easier to say, then. Did you know she's trying to get you replaced?"

"What?"

"Now, don't blame her. She's probably under orders from on high to save a few bucks on the budget. You know what they say, 'Never mix friendship with business.' You should hear her side of it before you tell her to drop dead."

"First," Hosato interrupted, "I think I should hear your side of it."

"Well," she began eagerly, "remember I said this was the second special problem I had to deal with this month? Well, the other one was her. She called me up last Thursday and said she wanted me to send out a personnel-scouting request to all our field agents. You'll never guess what for."

"A fencing coach?" Hosato supplied.

"Wrong," she said triumphantly. "For a spy! For someone who specializes in espionage and sabotage, *but*—and here's the kicker—a spy who can double as a fencing coach. It looks like someone thinks your job should be doing double duty. That's what hit me, you know. We used to have two girls here, one handling accounting problems and one covering personnel. Then . . ."

Hosato wasn't listening as she rambled on. The Ninja trap! So that's what Sasha had up her sleeve! Instead of proving the fencing coach had other talents, she was simply putting out a call for a list of dubious characters who could fence. All she would have to do would be to see if the existing coach were on it. If he were . . . Would it work? How many of his contacts would supply his name in response to that request? Would she make the connection between Hosato and Hayama? There were a lot of Japanese in space, but how many of them could fence?

"Hey!" The girl laid a hand on his arm, interrupting his thoughts.

"I didn't meant to get you upset. Even if she finds someone, you can always find another job, can't you?"

"Sure," he said bitterly. "As a professional duelist. I was trying to leave that behind. Not much job security, and the retirement plan is rotten."

"Gee, I'd like to run interference for you, but . . . well, you know, it's my job. Still," she said, "I do feel somehow responsible. Tell you what. I get off at four, why don't we get together over drinks, and maybe between the two of us we can come up with something."

"Okay." Hosato smiled. "Where shall I meet you?"

"Why don't I drop by your room?" she suggested. "And we can decide where we'll go from there."

Suzi will love that, he thought.

"Terrific," he said. "I'll see you then."

"Okay," she said, standing up. "And in the meantime, don't worry. Sasha's going to have her hands full for a while after what happened last night."

Hosato was suddenly alert.

"What happened last night?" he asked casually.

"Haven't you heard? Somebody killed Turner. Blew his head off with a blaster."

"What! Who did it?"

"Nobody knows, but it had to be one of the guards. They're the only ones in the complex with blasters. The president has ordered them all to turn in their weapons until the investigation is complete."

A spark burned in Hosato's memory. "Was he in the manufacturing area?"

"No, he was in his office. That's about all I know. See you after work." She started for the door.

"What about the boy? Turner's son. What happens to him?"

"Gee, I never thought about that. I suppose the company will take care of him somehow. See you later."

Hosato sat in thoughtful silence after she left. Finally he leaned forward and spoke into the desk-robot.

"Can you connect me with Harry Turner's personal quarters?"

"I can function as an intercom system," the robot responded.

"Then would you connect me, please?"

There was a silence; then James's voice came out of the speaker. "Yes?"

"Hayama here, James."

"Oh. Hayama. I won't be able to take my lesson today—"

"I know, I just heard. What I wanted to say was that after all this is over, if you're still interested, we can talk about your coming in with me as an apprentice."

"Thanks, Hayama. I appreciate that."

"One more thing, James. What was your father doing in his office last night?"

"It was the security-robot thing again. He was going to be looking at the first working prototypes."

12

"But you have my every assurance that such a thing is impossible!" Suzi floated at Hosato's heels as he paced up and down his apartment.

"Look, Suzi," Hosato said grimly, "I was almost killed twice yesterday by robots. How do you explain that?"

There was a moment of silence before the robot replied. "The only possible explanation is equipment malfunction."

"Twice? In the same area? Within fifteen minutes of each other?"

"The probability is admittedly low, but the possibility is still there," Suzi insisted. "Do you recall your arguments with my creator to program me so that I could attack with a fencing foil? It was safe, you said, there could be no injury so the programming would be acceptable. Do you recall what he said?"

"He said he wouldn't do it."

"He said he *couldn't* do it. Because you and I can converse like this, you keep forgetting one basic concept. Machines are dumb. That's why the base 'no-kill' programs are ingrained so deeply. A machine can't tell a blunted sword from a real one. If I were able to be programmed to fight with a mock weapon, you could then substitute a real weapon and I would kill with it. Our 'no-kill' programming therefore negates any such secondary programming."

There was a knock at the door.

"Please reconsider," Suzi begged. "The repercussions of your chosen action could—"

"No, Suzi," Hosato said and opened the door.

"Well, Hayama," Sasha said, sweeping briskly into the room. "What's the big emergency?"

"Sit down, Sasha." Hosato smiled. "This could take a while."

"No it won't," the security chief said coldly. "My entire force has been disarmed, the whole complex has gone crazy with accusations and suspicions, and I was supposed to be in the president's office five minutes ago. This won't take long at all."

"But this has to do with Turner's death," Hosato supplied.

"Fine. If you have information to give, then give it and let me get out of here."

Hosato sighed. "Look, Sasha. Will it slow you up at all if I say everything you've suspected about me is true? That I'm a Ninja?"

Sasha stopped abruptly and studied Hosato with dark eyes. "Did you kill Turner?" she asked softly.

"No, but I think I know who did . . . or *what* did, to be specific."

The security chief sank into a chair. "I'm listening," she announced. "I must say you've got the knack for getting my undivided attention."

"Before I get into my theory, there are a couple questions I want to ask you. As head of Security, any breach in an restricted area would be reported to you immediately, right?"

"That is correct."

"Aside from Harry Turner's death, were any other disturbances reported to you yesterday?"

"No."

"Specifically, in the manufacturing areas?"

"No. Why? Have you heard something—?"

"Next," Hosato interrupted, "is Turner's product family introducing any new robots that you know of?"

"That's a definite no." Sasha grimmaced. "They haven't come up with anything new in the last two years."

"Turner controls the Household line, doesn't he? Tell me, can you think of a household use for a rock slicer?"

Sasha frowned. "Not really. We use them in some of our construction robots, but slicers are too dangerous to be used around humans."

"How about blasters?"

"Look, Hayama. Enough games. If you have something to say, say it."

Hosato sighed and took the plunge.

"Okay. My name isn't Hayama, it's Hosato. By profession I am a Ninja, an advancement on the old-world model you've studied. I was hired by Ravensteel to infiltrate your complex for the express purpose of sabotage. I feel relatively safe admitting this to you, because so far I have done nothing except look around. I haven't killed anyone, destroyed any equipment, or transmitted any information to Ravensteel. My contract is now voided, but to my reasoning, the worst you can do is export me as an undesirable."

"That's quite a mouthful, Hayama . . . Hosato. The big question in my mind is, why?"

"For the money, of course."

"I mean, why tell me?"

"I'm coming to that." Hosato began to pace the room as he talked. "I'm breaking cover because I think there's something bigger at stake."

"Like what?"

"Killer robots. I think Harry Turner was killed by one of his own prototype security robots and that we're all in potential danger of sharing that fate."

"Whoa! Hold on, Hosato. Robot's can't—"

"Hear me out, Sasha. I mentioned I had done some looking around yesterday. I was specifically scouting Turner's manufacturing area for sabotage. I saw two things there that didn't make sense. First, the maintenance robots were constructing a new assembly line, yet you say there are no known new products planned for that area. Second, I saw a prototype robot being assembled with a built-in blaster in one arm and a light industrial slicer in the other."

"But robots can't kill people, they can't even injure them. Even if they have built-in weapons, they couldn't use them on anybody."

"In that same scouting trip, I was almost killed

twice, both times by robots. One time, one of the maintenance robots tried to knock me off a catwalk; and a few minutes later one of the design robots tried to shove a screwdriver through my chest. Does that sound like harmless robots going about their work?"

"It could be a malfunction," she suggested.

"That's what I thought at first myself. Then I found out that when Harry was killed, he was supposed to be looking over the prototypes of the security robots. It just seems like too much of a coincidence to me."

"But even if they were able to kill people, would robots have the necessary data to perform the function?"

"We can check that easily enough," Hosato said, turning to Suzi. "Suzi! We're going to need your help."

The robot remained stoically silent.

"Come on, Suzi. She knows already. There's no need for secrets anymore."

There was still no response.

"Am I to take it from your actions," Sasha asked, "that Suzi is more than the Class Two robot she's been pretending to be?"

"That's right," Hosato responded. "She's actually rather advanced. A Class Seven."

"Class Eight," Suzi corrected him.

"Ah." Hosato smiled. "Since you've decided to join us, what data are available to robots on the subject of killing?"

"Robots are incapable of killing or injuring humans," Suzi recited. "As any idiot knows."

Sasha snickered.

"That's right," Hosato said. "You all have 'no-kill' programming. But how do you know not to injure anyone?"

" 'No-kill' programming includes a complex matrix of human vulnerabilities," Suzi informed them. "We know the breaking strength of every bone in the body, modified for sex and age, the pressure necessary on what type of an edge to break the skin or rupture an internal organ, the sensitivities of the eyes or ears—"

"So you have all the information necessary to inflict injury. All robots do."

"The information is of a negative nature. These are things we are to avoid doing at all costs."

"But if the blocks were somehow removed, and you had programming to that effect, you would know precisely how to kill. Correct?"

There was a painful silence.

"You see, Sasha," Hosato said. "Robots could—"

"Even if we were physically able to inflict injury," Suzi interrupted, "there would have to be specific instruction to that effect before we could act. Robots are incapable of independent thought, and merely act out instructions given them."

"A mirror unto man," Sasha murmured.

"What's that?" Hosato asked.

"Oh. Just paraphrasing Shakespeare. The original quote was 'a mirror unto nature,' but that isn't what we're dealing with here. What we have is a mirror unto man, one that will reflect our efficiencies . . . and maybe our weaknesses."

"Then you agree that we could be in danger."

"No, I don't, Hosato." Sasha was her brisk self again. "While I'll admit it may be a possibility, there is nothing to prove—"

The shrill beeping of her belt unit interrupted her. She palmed the unit off her waist and held the ear plug against her head.

"Sasha here. . . . What? . . . Who is . . . ? Hello . . . Hello!"

Her hands sank slowly into her lap as she stared at Hosato.

"I think you've got your proof," she said vacantly. "While we've been here talking, someone or something raided the meeting in the president's office and killed everyone there. Security reports unidentified robots moving through the corridors, armed and capable of inflicting fatal injury."

13

Hosato grasped the situation immediately.

"Suzi," he barked. "Full battle equipment!"

The robot obediently pivoted around, and a door swung open.

"What . . . ?" began Sasha.

"Here. I assume you can use this," Hosato said, tossing her a blaster.

The security chief plucked it from the air and blinked at it. "I sure can. You're a bag of surprises, aren't you, Hosato?"

"I try," he said dryly, peeling off his shirt.

There was a knock at the door.

"I'll get it," Sasha volunteered.

"Watch it . . ." Hosato began, but she already had the door open.

The little redhead stood there. "Hi. I . . . Oh!"

Her glance took in Sasha and a half-naked Hosato at the same time. "Hey, if I'm interrupting anything, I—"

"Get in here, fast," Sasha ordered, beckoning with the blaster.

The girl obeyed, focusing on the blaster for the first time. "Hey! What's going on?"

"The robots are running amok and killing people. I know it sounds crazy, but. . . . What are you doing, Hosato?"

"What does it look like I'm doing? I'm changing clothes."

"I didn't know it mattered what you wore to an emergency."

"Take my word for it, it does." He continued don-ning his Ninja suit and produced another blaster from Suzi's depths.

"Here," he said, tossing it to the redhead. "Ever use one of these things?"

The redhead wrinkled her nose at the weapon. "No," she announced proudly.

"Well, honey, you're about to learn," Sasha said grimly.

"First things first," interrupted Hosato. "Get on your radio and alert your guards. Tell them to get to the armory and arm themselves as fast as they can. Then send a squad of them to secure the spaceport, and get the rest over here to guard the living quarters."

"I know how to do my job, Hosato," she snapped.

"Then do it!"

He reached for his room telephone and dialed hastily. "James? . . . Get over here to my room, fast. Don't ask questions, just do it. . . . That's right, and if you see any strange robots, avoid 'em like the plague. . . . Robots—it looks like your dad's security robot scheme has backfired. Just get over here fast!"

He slammed down the phone. "Suzi! Let's see those layout diagrams again!"

The robot pivoted, and once more the viewscreen blinked to life.

Hosato studied the drawings. "What's this?" he asked, pointing to an unlabeled outline, forgetting for a moment Suzi's limited powers of observation.

"That's the Maintenance Building," the redhead commented, peering over his shoulder. "Hey, that's a pretty neat robot. Who manufactures it?"

Hosato ignored her. "What's the story on the life-support systems, Suzi?" he asked.

"Life-support systems for the living quarters and mall are self-contained and independent of the main computer control. They are located at this point." An area of the layout diagram began to flash.

"Bad news, Hosato," Sasha interrupted. "The robots have the spaceport."

"Could someone tell me what's going on?" the redhead whined.

"What about the armory?"

"The robots have that, too," Sasha informed him. "My team managed to get some of the blasters out before the robots closed in, but not many. I've told them to pull back to the mall here to concentrate our forces."

There was a knock on the door.

"Stand back," Hosato hissed, motioning them away from the door.

With a fluid motion he rolled to the floor and lay, blaster ready, in front of the door.

"Who is it?" he called.

"James Turner," came the muffled response.

"Come on in, James," Hosato called back, his blaster never wavering.

The door burst open and the boy hurried into the room.

"There's firing in the . . ."

He stopped short, gaping at Hosato's blaster leveled at his midsection.

"Shut the door," Hosato ordered.

The boy groped behind him and closed the door, his eyes never leaving the blaster.

"Never mind Hosato," Sasha said briskly, stepping to his side. "He's a bit jumpy. We all are. What were you saying about firing?"

The boy gulped. "There's . . . somebody's firing blasters in the main corridor. The one leading to the rest of the complex."

Sasha swore absently. "That means they're on the way," she growled at last. "I'd better get down there and organize the defense."

"Wait a minute, Sasha," Hosato said, rolling to his feet. "Is there any other way out of the complex? One humans can use?"

"What?"

"Wake up. We can't hold them forever. They're probably manufacturing more while we're talking. We may have to evacuate the complex. Now, besides the spaceport, how can we get people out of here?"

Sasha thought for a moment. "I can't think of any—"

"How about the sand crawlers?" James interrupted. "The maintenance crews use them for gathering malfunctioning robots. They let me ride along with them a couple of times."

"How big are they and how many are there?"

"They can hold six, maybe ten in a pinch," Sasha supplied. "And there are only two of them."

Hosato grimaced. "It's not much, but it's all we've got. James, you and . . . What is your name, anyway?"

"Since you asked so nicely, it's Carolyn," the redhead retorted.

"Okay, you and Carolyn start going through the living quarters. Tell everybody to move down to the Maintenance Building. Don't take time to try to explain why, just tell them to do it and keep moving. Sasha will be organizing the corridor defense, and Suzi and I will go ahead to check the status on the sand crawlers. . . . Does that sound all right, Sasha?"

The last was added as he remembered his manners. He was starting to take command again.

"Sounds good to me," she replied, unruffled. "Do you have any more blasters to spare?"

"Just one, and that's mine," Hosato apologized.

She made a face at him. "Some spy. Well, let's go."

"Spy?" asked James, looking at Hosato.

"Later, James. Like the lady says, let's go."

The mall was a madhouse. Crowds of people were milling around in various stages of confusion and panic. Disembodied hands seemed to pluck at Hosato's sleeve as he and Suzi traversed the corridors. Voices babbled questions and demands at him, but he shrugged them off without breaking stride. The few who noticed he was carrying a blaster hurried to catch up with him, only to find his smooth pace deceptively fast.

Sasha had disappeared shortly after they left his room, but he assumed she was following her own route through the chaos. He could not waste energy worrying about her. She had her job and seemed competent enough to handle it. He had his. He had to make it to Maintenance, hopefully ahead of the crowds.

The narrow off-corridor to the Maintenance Building was unoccupied. Apparently no one else had recognized it as a possible avenue of escape. After the dimness of the mall, Hosato found the silence unnerving, and without realizing it, began carrying his blaster at the ready position.

The metal door at the end of the corridor was closed. A prickly, chilly sensation ran along Hosato's spine. He hesitated, then made his decision. He hadn't survived this long by ignoring his warning instincts. Motioning Suzi back against the wall, he bent and sealed his suit. Then, gripping his blaster, he reached out and jerked the door open.

The Maintenance Building was a wreck. Three men who had been huddled over something on the floor sprang apart and desperately dived for cover behind workbenches and boxes. As they scattered, Hosato saw they had been at work dismantling a security robot. Beyond it, several bodies lay on the floor.

"Who's there?" a shaky voice called out, and Hosato heard the quick scrabble as the man changed positions after speaking.

Stepping back into the corridor, out of their line of vision, Hosato broke the seals and rearranged his Ninja suit as he replied. "Hayama," he called. "I've got my robot with me, but she's stable and functioning normally."

"Come on ahead, Hayama," came a new voice Hosato recognized as Rick Handel's. "It's all right, you guys. I know him."

By the time Hosato reentered the room, two of the men had resumed their work with the fallen robot, leaving only Rick to greet him.

"Hayama, do you know anything about what the hell's going on?"

"I was just about to ask you. It looks like you've had a firsthand taste of the action here," Hosato observed. "All I know is, somehow Turner's security-robot plans backfired, and now we've got a pack of robots taking the place apart and killing anyone who crosses their path."

"Turner, huh? Well, that's one bit of information we didn't have. We got a call a while back that there were a couple of malfunctioning robots headed for the president's office . . . wouldn't respond to commands, they said. We sent a team out on the hustle, then got another call saying those 'bots had just broken into some high-level meeting and killed everybody in the place, including our section chief. We were trying to raise our team on the beepers to warn them off before they walked into a bad situation, when Mr. Personality there burst through the door and started burning everybody in sight."

He jerked his head toward the downed machine.

"Lucky for us, it could shoot in only one direction at a time, and it picked the wrong direction to start. Doc, there, has had some combat training and smashed in its front with a crescent wrench before any of the rest of us could move. We've been trying to find out what makes it tock instead of tick, but so far we can't figure it."

"Well, you haven't got much time," Hosato observed grimly. "The things are in the main corridor to the mall."

"Oh, lord!" Rick exclaimed, his eyes widening.

"That's right. Sasha and her security team are trying to stall them, but they can't hold them for long. We're trying to work out an evacuation plan, but we'll need your help. The spaceport's gone, so we'll have to use the sand crawlers. Where are they?"

"Through there." Rick pointed to a door at the rear of the shop. "There's an airlock at the far end of the garage that gives direct access to the surface area, but only one crawler is operational. The other one's half apart for preventive maintenance. It's scattered all over the garage."

"How fast could you put it back together?"

The mechanic gnawed at his lip. "Half an hour if I had some help," he said. "But—"

"Suzi," Hosato said, turning to his partner. "Go with Rick here and help him as much as you can."

"Hey, I can't take time to train a Class Two . . ."

"I am a Class Eight robot," Suzi replied coldly. "And am more than capable of following simple orders."

"A Class Eight?" Rick looked at her speculatively. "Say, Hayama, what are you doing with a Class Eight?"

"Sshh!" Hosato held up a hand for silence, then beckoned the mechanic closer.

"What's through that door?" he whispered, pointing to the ruined metal door at the side of the shop.

"The new corridor," Rick whispered back. "It runs past the main computer building and comes out—"

Hosato motioned him to silence again, and they listened. Coming from the door was the muffled whine of motors moving toward them down the corridor.

14

"Get to work on the sand crawler." Hosato whispered the order as he started sealing his Ninja suit.

"But what are you . . . ?" Rick began, then for the first time focused on the blaster in Hosato's hand. "Hey, where did you get the blaster? And what's with the funny outfit? Who are . . . ?"

Hosato finished sealing the suit and vanished.

"I suggest we do as he says," Suzi said to the stunned mechanic. "I'm sure he will explain later, if we get the time."

Hosato didn't delay to see the final resolution of Rick's dilemma. He moved across the room in a smooth glide and stepped through the ruined doorway into the corridor.

There were three of them moving slowly down the corridor. He had never seen a robot try to "sneak" but guessed this was their attempt to duplicate that form of motion. At these speeds, their motors were next to noiseless. If Hosato had not already been alerted and nervous, it is doubtful he would have heard them at all.

Instead of opening fire immediately, Hosato took a moment to plan his attack. In theory, he should have nothing to fear. His suit gave him invisibility and therefore invulnerability. If the robots' camera eyes did not register a human form, they would not fire. Even his blaster was rigged to establish contact through his palm, and shared the same light-relay mechanism as his suit. He was totally invisible and safe—in theory. Of course, relying on theories was a sure way to guarantee an early retirement.

There was always the possibility that cameras were not the robots' sole means of sensory input. Heat sensors, movement detectors, any one of a number of devices could detect his presence, and then he would be in a shoot-out with three machines that didn't miss.

The robots were a scant fifteen feet away. His plan of action set, Hosato opened fire.

Standing off-center to the right of the corridor, he fired point-blank at the lead robot. Dropping to one knee, he fired again immediately at the robot at the rear of the formation. Not waiting to observe the results of his first two shots, he dived to his left, rolling to the side of the corridor, and from a prone position fired again at the final robot.

He rolled again, still prone, to the center of the corridor, and froze, studying his targets. Observing no sign of continued activity from the robots, he drew a deep breath and waited for his heartbeat to return to its normal pacing. Realization suddenly struck him. Between his second and third shots, the last robot had returned fire, the bolt from its blaster sizzling the air over Hosato as he rolled across the corridor.

He shot a quick glance behind him to check his retreat route. The smoldering body of a security guard lay just inside the door.

That's what the robot had fired at! It was reacting to the security guard's intrusion into the corridor. Had Hosato been on his feet, he would have been caught in the line of fire, invisible or not!

He suddenly saw another blaster being poked cautiously into the corridor, a blaster held by a hand with a uniform sleeve showing.

"Hold your fire!" he called, quickly breaking the seal on his suit.

He rolled to his feet and confronted the bewildered guard who cautiously followed the blaster into the corridor.

"How did you—?" the guard began.

"How do we get into the main computer building?" Hosato demanded.

"We can't!" the guard responded automatically.

"Look, don't you understand?" Hosato pressured. "If we can knock out that computer, the robots will be minus a brain. That's where they're being controlled from."

The guard's face hardened. "That's a top-security area," he recited. "Orders state that unauthorized personnel—"

Hosato almost hit the man in his frustration but gained control of himself.

"Where's Sasha?" he demanded. "We'll get your orders changed right now."

"The chief's been hurt," the guard informed him. "Just before we collapsed the main tunnel, she . . ."

But Hosato was gone, pushing his way into the maintenance shop. Chaos reigned in the shop. There were people packed into every available space, all shouting at each other. Bits of conversation came to Hosato as he made his way through the crowd.

". . . it's got to be the main programming. They couldn't just . . ."

". . . has been in the family for two hundred years, and you just . . ."

". . . the brains God gave an ant, you'd quite poking around in the mechanics and help us figure . . ."

". . . Billy . . . Billy . . . Maria, have you seen . . . ?"

". . . long until they burn a new corridor, we've got to . . ."

He found her at last. She was lying on the floor. James was trying to keep the crowd from stepping on her, but with limited success.

"Hosato!" the boy cried, spying him as he covered the final distance through the press of bodies. "Sasha's—"

"I heard," he said, dropping to one knee beside the fallen security chief. "How is she?"

It was a rhetorical question, and he ignored the boy's answer as he took in the situation at a glance. Sasha's right arm was gone below the elbow. There was no bleeding, probably cauterized by the same blaster bolt that took her arm, but she was in deep shock.

"Carolyn's dead," James shouted in Hosato's ear.

"Who?" he replied absently.

"Carolyn. The red-headed girl in your room. When we were . . ."

Someone, pushed backward by the crowd, walked directly across Sasha's body. Hosato pushed savagely at the legs, then stood up, casting about desperately. A familiar face caught his eye.

"Doc!" he called.

The maintenance man was embroiled in an argument with a red-faced couple and didn't respond. Hosato stretched out, got hold of his arm, and physically dragged him out of the conversation.

"We've got an injured person down here, Doc. Is there someplace we can take her where she won't get trampled?"

"Try the garage. Rick chased everybody out of there while he was working on the crawler."

"Thanks!" Hosato said, releasing his hold on the mechanic.

"Say," the man asked, "are you headed back there?"

Hosato was scanning the crowd, trying to pick a path. "Yes," he replied absently.

"Can you take these to Rick?" the man said, forcing a wad of papers into Hosato's hand. "Maybe he can make head or tails of them."

"Sure," Hosato acknowledged. "Come on, James."

He stooped and picked Sasha up in his arms. Even with James breaking a path through the crowd, it was hard maneuvering. The door to the garage was worst of all. There were so many people in front of it Hosato had to momentarily set Sasha down and physi-

cally shove people away before he could get it open.
As it was, he and James barely got Sasha through before the jostling crowd slammed the door shut behind
them.

"I told you to stay out of . . . Oh, Hayama." Rick
emerged from under the sand crawler he was working
on. "What's . . . ? Oh, my God!"

"She'll be okay," Hosato said, easing his burden to
the ground. "How's the work going?"

"Nearly complete," Suzi pronounced, gliding into
view from the far side of the crawler. "Another five
minutes of uninterrupted work and the vehicle will
be fully functional."

"That's right," Rick confirmed. "That's quite a 'bot
you have there, Hayama. I'm going to have a whole
shipload of questions for you when all this is over, but
in the meantime . . ."

"Right," Hosato responded. "I'll get out of your
way. Oh . . ." He suddenly realized he was still holding the wad of papers. "Here, Doc, said you should
take a look at these."

The mechanic took the bundle and frowned at it.
"What are they?"

"I don't know," Hosato admitted. "Doc just said—"
Their heads came around with a jerk. Muffled
screams, mixed with the unmistakable sound of
blaster fire, were coming from the door.

"My God," Rick gasped. "They're in the shop."

"James! Get Sasha into the crawler. That one, the
one that's working. Suzi! Give him a hand."

Hosato turned to Rick and lowered his voice. "Get
this thing fired up and ready to roll. I'll see if there's
anything we can do."

Rick nodded and darted toward the controls of the
working sand crawler, and Hosato turned toward the
door.

The screams were redoubling. Unseen fists were
pounding at the door to the garage. In a flash, Hosato
realized what was happening. The door opened into

the shop, and the panicked people were shoving against it, prevented by their own numbers from getting it open.

With a curse he ran to the door and threw his weight against it. Then he backed up and launched a flying double kick into the door.

The door didn't budge an inch.

Hammering on the door, he tried shouting instructions to the people on the other side. Finally he stopped, realizing the futility of his actions. Simultaneously he realized the screams from the shop were dying out, replaced by eerie silence and the sporadic sound of blasters.

He turned and sprinted for the crawler, fighting back the cold, sick feeling in his stomach.

15

Hanging over Rick's shoulder, Hosato peered curiously at the piloting viewscreen as the sand crawler jolted its way across the rough terrain.

"How far is it to the Ravensteel complex?" he asked, swaying as the crawler plunged down another gully.

"Not far," Rick assured him. "I've never been there myself, but I know we're working opposite ends of the same mineral vein. I figure we should be there by morning . . . noon tomorrow at the latest."

Hosato squinted skeptically at the viewscreen. "That's pretty rough terrain out here."

"Don't worry. This baby's built to run over this stuff."

Rick's faith in the vehicle seemed to be well-founded. It was like an exaggerated version of a tank —no, tanks had caterpillar treads, and this had huge balloon tires, eight of them, with independent suspension. More like a large version of an armored car. It was short and wide, with the rectangular crew housing perched in the center. Mounted forward of the housing was a pair of large pincer-arms as well as a small forest of lesser tool arms. The arms could be controlled from the driver's seat with amazing dexterity and strength. The area to the rear of the housing was taken up by a small airlock that gave the operators access to the outside, should the work require the human touch. It was an impressive machine, but it was still a machine.

"Are you sure the main computer can't take control of this thing?" Hosato asked nervously.

"Impossible," Rick assured him.

"If you don't mind my being blunt, that's what everyone said about the idea of killer robots. Impossible, but it happened anyway."

Rick sighed. "Look, are you worried about Suzi running amok?"

"No, but—"

"Well, there's more chance of her being dominated by the computer than there is of this crawler being affected."

Hosato shot a glance through the low door to the crew area, where James and Suzi were hovering over Sasha.

"Now, I didn't mean you should get paranoid about Suzi," Rick chided. "Look, Suzi's capable of independent action, but she has no capacity for computer direction. And this crawler has no capacity for computer direction, and it isn't capable of independent action. The only controls for this baby are right here in my hand, so don't worry."

Hosato hesitated a moment, but decided the embarrassment of admitting his ignorance was worth the information to be gained. "How does that differ from what happened back at the complex?" he asked.

"The security robots are like most of the robots we use: run by one central computer. They are free-moving, multifunction robots, but the decision-making and function cues were still left in the central computer."

He stopped talking to concentrate on piloting the vehicle around a rock formation.

"So all the killer robots were being controlled from the central computer?" Hosato prompted, once the obstacle had been cleared.

"That's right," Rick confirmed. "Their activities were too complex and unified to be self-directed. The problem isn't with the individuals units, it's with the central computer."

Hosato swore.

"What's wrong?" his friend asked.

"I had a chance to go after the central computer and passed it up. If I could have gotten to it—"

"—you wouldn't be here," Rick interrupted. "Sasha could probably tell you more about it than I can, but believe me, that thing's protected. You don't just walk up and turn it off. Incidentally, how is she doing back there, anyway?"

"I'll check," said Hosato, and ducked back to the crew area.

Sasha was lying on the floor, her eyes open. Her listless thrashing about constantly threatened to displace the blankets they had heaped on her.

"How is she doing?" Hosato asked.

James turned worried eyes up to him. "We're trying to keep her covered, but she keeps—"

"They'll burn through!" Sasha moaned suddenly, sitting up. "We need a bigger block! Collapse another twenty feet—"

"It's all right, Sasha," Hosato soothed, taking her by her shoulders and easing her back down.

"You don't understand." She turned vacant eyes to him. "They'll burn through. We've got to stop them."

"They're stopped," he assured her. "Everything's all right. Get some rest, now."

"Hosato?" She blinked at him. "Could you get a doctor? I think my right hand's hurt. The fingers feel like they're on fire."

She tried to raise her right arm to look at it, but Hosato restrained her.

"Just get some rest. Everything will be all right."

"Hayama! Come up here, quick!"

Hosato was momentarily torn by indecision.

"Take care of her, James," he said finally, relinquishing his hold to the boy and starting forward.

"We've got problems," Rick announced grimly as Hosato entered the pilot's booth. "Watch the rear viewscreen there as we hit the top of this next rise."

Hosato did as he was told. The moon was bright enough to throw shadows as he surveyed the scene in the viewscreen. At first he saw nothing; then something moved in the center of the screen. A blob detached itself from a patch of shadows, then was obscured from sight as their crawler plunged into the next gully.

"What is it?" he asked tensely.

"The central computer's sent one of the ore scouts after us."

"What can it do?"

"Well, it's got an industrial slicer as one of its tools, and an ore crane for another. It can pick us up or cut us apart, depending on its instructions. From what happened back at the complex, my guess is it'll cut us apart."

"Hosato!" James called from the back. "Can you give me a hand here?"

"In a minute, James," Hosato called back.

"Say, I've been meaning to ask," Rick said. "Is it Hayama or Hosato? The kid there keeps—"

"It's Hosato. Can that thing catch us?"

"It's faster than we are, but we're almost out of range of the computer's control radius."

"Good." Hosato sighed.

"Not so fast," Rick retorted. "I said 'almost.' We've got another half-hour's driving before we're clear. It'll be close, but it'll probably catch us. Even if it doesn't, it'll be close enough to use its slicer on us."

Hosato studied the pursuing vehicle as it came into view again.

"Where are the surface suits?" he asked finally.

"In the tall lockers back in the crew area. Why?" But Hosato was already gone.

"Hosato—" the boy began, looking up.

"Not now, James," Hosato mumbled, brushing past him. "We've got problems."

"If I might suggest . . ." Suzi began, but Hosato ignored the robot.

"If anything happens, James," he said, dragging the bulky surface suit from the locker and gathering it in his arms, "get in touch with the Hungarian. Suzi can tell you how to find him."

"But—"

Hosato cut him short, calling ahead to Rick as he started for the cockpit again.

"Stop the crawler in the next gully!"

"What for?" the mechanic called back.

"We haven't got time to argue," Hosato growled, joining him in the cockpit. "Just stop this thing and help me get into this suit."

"What are you going to do?"

"I'm going to take a blaster and lay a little ambush for our friend there."

"You're nuts," Rick proclaimed. "You won't stand a chance out there."

"If I don't, none of us have a chance. At least I can create a diversion until the rest of you are out of range. Now, stop this thing."

The mechanic obediently pulled the vehicle to a halt in the dark shadows of a gully.

"All right," he said, swiveling in his chair to help Hosato with the suit, "but how will we know to come back and pick you up?"

"You don't," Hosato replied, struggling with the suit's fastenings. "You get out of range and wait. If this works, I'll follow your tracks and catch up with you. If I'm not there by sunrise, I'm not coming."

"Well, good luck, Hosato." Rick slapped him on the back as he headed back to the crew area.

Just through the doorway, he stopped suddenly. His swords, his clothes, were all heaped in the center of the floor next to James. It took him a moment to realize the implications of this fact; then he cast about the area, opening his faceplate.

"Where's Suzi?" he demanded.

"She . . . she told me to unload her," James stammered.

"But where is she?" Hosato barked.

As if in response, he heard a muffled hiss of compressed air. The outer airlock door had just opened.

16

Hosato stooped and rummaged desperately through his gear.

"I didn't know what she was going to do!" the boy insisted. "All of a sudden she was gone."

Hosato finally found what he was looking for. The radio unit he and Suzi sometimes used for communications. Thumbing the unit on, he raised it quickly to his lips.

"Suzi!" he called. "What are you doing?"

"What's going on?" Rick called from the cockpit.

Hosato pushed his way forward again, centering his attention on the rear viewscreen.

"See for yourself!" he said, nodding at the screen.

Suzi could be seen clearly, steadfastly making her way back along the crawler's tracks.

"If you don't mind my saying so," Rich said archly, "that's a waste of a fine robot. She can't do anything against that ore scout."

"I didn't send her," Hosato snarled. "She's out there on her own."

The robot was almost out of sight as Hosato thumbed the radio button again.

"Suzi. I asked you a direct question. Respond!"

"I am executing your plan for diversionary action," came the calm reply.

"The plan was for *me* to create a diversion," Hosato barked.

"That was the only flaw in your plan. I am eminently better suited than you for this mission."

"Return to the crawler at once!"

"May I remind you"—Suzi's voice was dry, despite

the radio—"the purpose of this maneuver is to gain time for the crawler to escape. That effect will very quickly be lost if you continue to delay your departure. The time for argument is past."

"She's right," Rick said, and set the crawler in motion again.

Hosato started to stop him, then hesitated. Suzi was right—at least on the time element. Then again, if she failed, he could still try his own gambit.

"For the record," he said into the radio, "I disagree with your assertion that you can deal with the ore scout better than I could."

"Normally you would be correct," Suzi retorted, "but under surface conditions my mobility and maneuverability exceed your own."

"But your programming won't allow you to carry out any aggressive functions. How do you expect to stop it?"

"Even though I cannot pose an actual threat, if the ore scout perceives me as a threat, it'll stop."

"And then it will start again and you'll be dead."

"Actually, the correct phrase is 'nonfunctional.' "

Hosato was involuntarily startled by the correction. He realized suddenly that he had grown to think of Suzi not as a robot but as a living individual.

"Suzi—" he began slowly.

"Future communications will occur only as time permits," the robot's voice interrupted. "The ore scout is in sight now."

Hosato waited impatiently for the crawler to top another rise, thereby giving him a view of the action occurring to their rear. But as the scene rose into the viewscreen, he could see nothing. Then, as they were about to plunge into the next gully, there was a quick flash of light.

The ore scout had fired its slicer. Apparently the two robots were somewhere in one of the gullies, hidden from the crawler's line of sight.

As their vehicle reached the bottom of the gully, the

front viewscreen picked up a second flash of light reflected on the ridge ahead. The slicer had been fired a second time.

"Suzi!" Hosato called into the radio. "Are you all right?"

"It missed," replied the robot.

"How are you drawing its fire?"

"Just a minute."

There was another flash of light.

Hosato waited. There was no sound from the radio.

"Suzi?"

Silence.

"Suzi?" he repeated.

"In response to your question," came Suzi's voice, "I am playing upon the machine's target-image sensitivities."

Relief flooded over Hosato, but he kept it out of his voice. "Could I have that last bit in English?" he asked.

"From the actions displayed by the security robots at the complex, it is apparent they are being directed by the central computer to seek out and destroy objects of a humanoid form. That means the target image must display cerain properties of shape—specifically, a head, a given body shape . . . Excuse me a moment."

There was another flash of light.

"Suzi! What are you doing?" Hosato barked.

"That is what I am attempting to explain," came the calm response. "Additional questions will only prolong my efforts."

Hosato ground his teeth. He had dealt with Suzi's explanations before. They were usually drawn out and detailed, but it was useless to try to rush her.

"Sorry, Suzi." He sighed. "But could you try to keep it to the major points only?"

"I never indulge in needless . . . Excuse me."

There was another flash of light.

"Whatever she's doing, it's keeping that thing pinned down," Rick commented.

Hosato nodded absently, waiting for Suzi to continue her oration.

"As I was saying," Suzi's voice came again, "fortunately I have been provided with just such a shape— or half of one, to be specific. It seems to be sufficient to convince the ore scout's scanners that I am a target."

For a moment Hosato was confused, but then he remembered. The fencing manikin! By facing the fencing manikin with its single arm toward the ore scout, she was making it believe she was a human!

"We'll be out of range soon," Rick announced.

Hosato ignored him. The information was welcome, but at the moment his attention was commanded by Suzi's report.

"By presenting the humanoid shape," Suzi was saying, "I am able to draw the ore scout's attention and activate its attack pattern. Then, by removing the image, I am able to effectively disappear as a target. Apparently the scout is directed to search for the target for a given period of time before resuming its pursuit of the sand crawler. The periodic interruptions in my transmission occur when the scout starts to abandon its search, thereby making it necessary to display the target once more. Excuse me."

It occurred to Hosato that Suzi was flirting with disaster. The slicer would destroy her completely if it touched her even once. If she were slow in turning, or . . .

"Suzi!" he said desperately. "Do you know if the central computer has a learning capacity? If it does, a repeated pattern could be detected and the target image changed."

"That's right!" Rick supplied. "The computer *does* have that capacity."

"Even if that capacity exists," Suzi's reply came,

"in my opinion it has not received sufficient data to effect such a change."

A warning bell went off in Hosato's mind: Something that had been drilled into his head time and time again during his training.

"Suzi!" he warned. "Never underestimate your opponent. Don't make plans that hinge on his incompetence or inability to react."

There was no response.

"Suzi?" he repeated.

"We're out of range now," Rick said over his shoulder.

"Suzi? Status check!"

Silence.

"Shall I stop and wait for the robot?" Rick asked.

Hosato didn't reply.

"I said, shall I—"

"No," said Hosato, his hand holding the silent radio dropping listlessly to his side. "There's no use waiting. Push on for Ravensteel."

"We've got to stop them!"

Sasha's delirious moanings from the crew area echoed Hosato's own thoughts.

17

"That's an interesting story, Hosato."

The Ravensteel security chief's tone matched his indolent sprawl in the office chair.

Hosato's alarm and annoyance with the situation grew. Something was wrong. He had realized that when their arrival at Ravensteel was met by armed guards, guards who had not lowered their weapons when Hosato announced who he was and his affiliation with Ravensteel.

"That's my report," he corrected. "If you'll get in touch with one of the executives in charge of this mission, I'll be glad to repeat it for him."

"I've already contacted those parties." The man smiled. "They've delegated full authority in this matter to me."

Hosato was suddenly aware again of the armed guard standing behind his chair. "Very well, then," he said with forced casualness. "What else do you want to know?"

The man, Gedge, leaned forward and rested his elbows on his desk. "You could start by explaining what it is you want from Ravensteel."

Hosato was stunned by the statement. "I . . . I don't understand," he managed at last.

"Oh, come now, Hosato." Gedge winked knowingly. "What are you after, really? More money?"

Hosato reminded himself again of the guard and held his temper in check.

"Actually," he said levelly, "I had the ridiculous idea Ravensteel might be interested in helping. It would be in their best interest, you know."

Gedge's gaze never wavered, and neither did his smile.

"Ravensteel is interested only in pleasing its customers and its stockholders," he recited.

"All of whom are human," Hosato supplied. "Perhaps I didn't make myself clear. The robots are killing all humans—women, children, everybody. I don't see any reason why Ravensteel would be exempted, unless . . ."

A thought suddenly occurred to him. This man was far too unruffled and sure of himself.

". . . unless Ravensteel is controlling them," he finished thoughtfully.

Gedge dropped his eyes and chuckled to himself.

"Hosato," he said, reestablishing eye contact, "you're really quite amusing. Now, tell me, what are we supposed to be controlling them to do?"

Hosato's anger flashed. "I've been telling you!" he snarled. "To—"

"—run amok and kill people," Gedge interrupted. "That's right, I keep forgetting."

His eyes hardened, and he half-rose from his desk as he glared at Hosato. "I keep forgetting because it isn't true! McCrae Enterprises is functioning today as normally as it was yesterday and the day before."

"What?" Hosato exclaimed.

"That's right, Hosato. We checked your story, ridiculous as it was. McCrae is taking orders, making shipments, and conducting tours just like they always have."

"But that's impossible!"

"You'd think so, wouldn't you?" Gedge smiled. "At the very least, it makes a rather substantial contradiction to your story."

"Wait a minute," Hosato began excitedly. "It's the robots. It's got to be. Has anyone human from McCrae been in contact with the outside world since yesterday?"

"As a matter of fact, we tried. Would you like to see the tapes?"

Gedge keyed a reference number into his desk-robot and swiveled the viewscreen so Hosato could watch. The very human features of a uniformed Mc-Crae security guard blinked into view.

"Security," the face said briskly.

"Gedge from Ravensteel here," came Gedge's voice. "Let me talk with Sasha."

"She is unavailable," the guard responded. "May I be of assistance?"

"Perhaps," Gedge's voice continued smoothly. "One of our ore scouts malfunctioned and got away from us. The last time we saw it, it was headed your way. We'd like permission to cross over onto your property and reclaim it."

"Under no circumstances are Ravensteel personnel allowed on McCrae property," the guard recited. "We will conduct a search of our own and notify you of the results."

"I want to talk to Sasha," Gedge insisted stubbornly. "She'd let us—"

"She is on a priority mission at this time," the guard interrupted. "Until her return, I am in temporary command. McCrae rules are very specific on the point of trespassers. We will conduct our own search, and if any Ravensteel personnel are found on McCrae property, they will be fired on as saboteurs."

The screen blinked out as the guard broke the connection.

"That doesn't prove anything," Hosato insisted. "You know as well as I do, transmissions and displays can be phonied electronically. Hell, Suzi could do that!"

"Who? Oh, yes, your robot. Well, I don't know much about that. Your people were always better than us at radios and transistors and stuff like that."

The casual dismissal in his voice gave more impact

to the racial slur than would have been gained with sarcasm.

"But what it comes down to, Hosato, is, I don't believe your cock-and-bull story. More importantly, neither does the executive board. We think you sold out to McCrae."

A tiny spark of fear replaced Hosato's anger. He began to wonder if he would be alive at the end of his meeting.

"How am I supposed to have sold out?" he asked quietly.

"You're good, Hosato. I'll admit that. A specialist." Gedge waved a casual hand at Hosato's gear and weapons arrayed on his desk. "Did you know that any one of a dozen on my team would have tried your mission? For no extra pay? No, you probably wouldn't. You're the outside specialist they went to instead."

Hosato was about to repeat his question, then held his silence.

"Fifteen thousand with no results guaranteed." Gedge shook his head in mock admiration. "I don't mind admitting, Hosato, I'd be willing to do nothing for a lot less than that."

He laughed at his own joke before continuing.

"So there you were, no loyalties to Ravensteel, no career to worry about, nothing to inspire you to finish the mission except more money. Now, the McCrae security system is tight, maybe the best except for ours. There's no way you could crack that system without risking your life, and with fifteen thousand in your pocket, why should you?"

Hosato thought of his family's generations-long record of successful missions, but kept his silence.

"Now, here's where I take my hat off to you, Hosato." Gedge smiled. "Ninety-nine out of a hundred space bums would have taken the money and run, but not you. You saw a way to squeeze a few more credits out of the situation. You reveal yourself to McCrae, and offer to use your position with Ravensteel to get a spy through the door—not just *a* spy, but their own chief of security!"

Hosato forced a smile. "I suppose it doesn't make an impression on anyone that she's had her arm blown off."

"That was a nice touch," Gedge admitted. "It almost worked, until I reminded the board that Sasha would probably let you cut off both her legs to get an inside look at Ravensteel security."

"I see," Hosato said thoughtfully.

"So the only question left is, how much did they pay you, or, more important, how much will it cost to get you back on our side?"

Hosato met his eyes and smiled. For a brief moment anger flashed in Gedge's ice-blue eyes; then it was gone.

"You're a brassy bastard!" He laughed, shaking his head. "I think it's safe to say the board will probably go along with it, especially since you brought them a present."

"How's that?"

"Sasha, of course." Gedge winked again. "She was your ace in the hole all along. She has enough data on McCrae security in her head to keep my team busy for a long time. I don't know how you got her to go along with this, but bringing her with you gives you the leverage you need to change sides again. Sheer brilliance."

Hosato shrugged modestly and stood up, extending his hand. "Well," he said, "I tried. It's good to be working for Ravensteel again."

Gedge ignored his hand. "When will you be ready to start?" he asked. "As soon as we get the information out of Sasha, I assume."

"Actually"—Hosato smiled—"I won't have to wait that long. I've gotten most of the data I need. Just keep her here and away from McCrae until I'm done. Incidentally"—he shot a glance around the room—

"what did you do with the other two? The kid and the mechanic."

"We're holding them next door." Gedge gestured at the door in the wall. "We weren't sure if we should kick 'em off-planet or just kill them."

"Keep 'em," Hosato advised. "They'll make good hostages."

"Hey, that's a good idea," Gedge admitted. "Say, what is that thing, anyway?"

Hosato had started to pick up his gear from the desk.

"This?" he asked, holding up a six-inch metal rod with a sharp point.

"Yeah. Is it a poison injector or a climbing spike or what?"

Hosato smiled. "Actually, it's much simpler than that," he confided. "It works like this."

As he spoke, he released the throwing spike with a sharp snap of his wrist. The spike darted across the room and embedded half its length in the forehead of the watching guard.

18

A surprised look spread across the guard's face; then he crumpled to the floor.

Gedge blinked, then started to turn to Hosato.

An épée was in Hosato's hand, and a gleam of light from the overhead lamp shone from its needle point, hovering inches from Gedge's throat.

"Don't even twitch, Gedge," he said coldly. "There aren't many reasons for keeping you alive, and lots for killing you. All I need is an excuse to change my mind."

Gedge swallowed hard but kept his voice level. "What . . . ? What's your game, Hosato?"

"That's the problem," Hosato retorted. "You've got it into your head I'm out to destroy Ravensteel. Well, that's your prerogative. It's mine not to go along with it."

Gedge licked his lips nervously. "Okay, Hosato. Put the sword away and let's talk it out."

"No deal. Now we play it my way." He edged over to the fallen guard and retrieved the blaster, shifting the sword to his left hand.

"How many guards on the two next door?" he demanded.

"Look, Hosato, we can—"

"*How many?*"

"Two."

Hosato moved sideways until he stood against the wall beside the door into the adjoining room.

"If you're lying, Gedge, you'll be the first to go. Now, open the door and call to them."

Gedge hesitated, then moved to the door and opened it.

"We've got a code Delta," he announced casually.

In a flash Hosato was in the doorway, his blaster leveled at the occupants of the next room.

"Freeze!" he snarled.

The two guards, hands on the butts of their blasters, froze in place. Rick and James were seated on a sofa against the far wall, apparently unharmed. Hosato noted with satisfaction they had failed to relieve James of his dress sword—probably didn't consider it a serious weapon.

"All right, toss your blasters into the corner," he instructed the guards. "Easy!"

The guards obeyed with leaden slowness.

"Nice try, Gedge," Hosato commented to his captive as the blasters thudded into the corner. "I don't know what a code Delta is, but I had a hunch I wouldn't like it. Okay, Rick, get their—"

Gedge kicked the door shut on his arm and rushed him.

Fighting the pain of his pinned arm, Hosato hammered at his assailant with the bell guard of his épée. Gedge was inside the length of the sword, negating the use of the point, and he clung to Hosato tenaciously for several precious seconds.

Finally Hosato slammed the heavy pommel against the larger man's temple, and Gedge sagged, his grip loosening. With a heave Hosato shoved the man off him and wrenched the door open.

In the corner, Rick was wrestling with one of the guards, apparently for possession of one of the blasters. Before Hosato could call out, the mechanic found the proper leverage and jerked his opponent's head around sharply. There was an audible crack, and the guard went limp.

The other guard was . . . Hosato hesitated as he focused for the first time on the prostrate form on the floor by his feet. There was a pool of blood slowly spreading from the body.

James was standing shakily nearby, his bloody dress sword hanging limply in his hand.

Their eyes met.

"He . . . he was going to . . ."

"It's all right now, James," Hosato said quietly.

"I . . . killed him."

"You sure did, kid," Rick interrupted. "Saved your hide, too, Hosato. What do we do now?"

Hosato felt a quick surge of anger at Rick's callousness; then it subsided. Rick was right. This was a time for action.

"Are you all right, James?" he asked brusquely, taking the boy by the shoulder.

The youth blinked vacantly, then nodded his head in stubborn assent.

"Rick, get their blasters."

Without waiting for the mechanic's reply, Hosato turned and strode into Gedge's office once more. The security chief was conscious but out of action. He was hunched over on his hands and knees, holding his head and moaning softly. Hosato ignored him and moved to the desk, arming himself from his own arsenal, which Gedge had so conveniently laid out for him.

As he had noted earlier, his blasters were gone. Well, no matter. They'd gotten new ones from the guards. Throwing spikes in his belt, knife in his boot . . . One by one he secured the deadly tools of his trade at various points on his body. Items such as clothing, he ignored. This was a combat mission.

"I've got the blasters, Hosato," Rick said, joining him. "Now what?"

Hosato gestured at Gedge's huddled form. "Ask our friend there where they took Sasha."

Rick frowned. "I don't think he'll tell me."

"They've taken her off to interrogate her," Hosato informed him. "Thinking about that might help you find the right way to ask him."

"Right!" Rick said, his face hardening.

Hosato felt a twinge of guilt as he turned his back on the inevitable scene in the corner. He shouldn't delegate such a task to someone else, but forcing information out of people, especially injured people, had never been his forte. Still, he winced at Gedge's first gasp of pain.

"Hosato?"

He turned, to find James at his side.

"I had to do it," the boy mumbled. "He was going to kill you."

Hosato seized the boy's shoulders in an iron grip and shook him. "You said you wanted to come with me, James. Remember?"

"Yes, but—"

"Well, this is what I do. I kill people. We may have to kill some more before we get out of here. If we don't, they'll kill us. I'm not saying you should like it, but accept it. Accept it now, or when the next time comes, you'll hesitate and we'll all be dead."

The boy's eyes cleared. "I'll be all right," he said levelly.

"You're sure?"

"Yes." His voice was surer now.

"Good. Then fetch my throwing spike. It's in the guard's forehead over there."

It was a brutal thing to do, and Hosato watched the boy covertly as he went about his assignment. The boy was a bit wooden-limbed, but his hands shook only slightly as he withdrew the weapon from the corpse's skull.

"I've got your answer, Hosato," Rick called. "Sasha is in the room directly below us. The stairs are across the hall."

"Here's your spike," James said, passing him the weapon.

Hosato took it absently and tucked it in his belt.

"Shall I kill him?" Rick asked, jerking his head at Gedge.

"No. Hang on to him. He's our hostage for now."

"Okay, you're the boss. Where do we go from here?"

"*I* go after Sasha," Hosato corrected. "You try to find if one of these uniforms comes close to fitting you. James."—Hosato pressed a blaster into the boy's hand —"watch the door. If anybody but me or Sasha comes through it, kill 'em. And keep an eye on our friend there."

Their eyes met; then the boy smiled and nodded.

There was no one in sight as Hosato ghosted across the corridor and down the stairs. Likewise, there was no one in the lower corridor, not even a guard.

His suspicions aroused, he crossed the corridor in one long stride and hurtled himself against the door. It flew open with surprising ease, and he fell headlong into a dark room. As he hit the floor, he realized what a beautiful target he made silhouetted against the open door, and rolled sideways into the shadows.

"Hosato?" came a cautious call.

"Sasha?" he answered.

There was a soft shuffle of movement, and the door closed behind him. A moment later the lights came on, flooding the scene in the room with their harsh brilliance.

"I'll say one thing for you, Hosato. You never miss a chance to make a big entrance."

Sasha was standing there, a blaster gripped loosely in her left hand. Aside from her disheveled appearance, she seemed unharmed.

"Are you all right?" Hosato asked, rolling to his feet.

"Sure," she replied easily. "Nothing like the smell of truth serum to clear away the cobwebs. Luckily they didn't seem to think I was dangerous enough to strap down." She gestured at the two crumpled and bloody forms on the floor.

Hosato whistled in silent appreciation.

"It looks like they were wrong in the worst way. How did you do it?"

"With my trusty desk lamp," Sasha replied modestly, pointing at the implement. "You know, they ought to outlaw those things. They're dangerous."

"I meant, how did you do it at all?"

Sasha shot an annoyed glance at him. "By taking the one with the blaster first. After that, the other one was easy. I'm surprised you didn't know that, Hosato."

"As a matter of fact, I am familiar with that tactic," Hosato retorted. "But when I do it, it's neater."

Sasha shook her head and held up her blaster. "Okay, Hosato. If we're done rattling our sabers at each other, maybe we can get a few basic questions answered. For one, where the hell are we? Last thing I remember, I was fighting robots at the main corridor, then I wake up here with Dr. Frankenstein there about to shoot a load of goop into me."

Hosato shook his head. "McCrae isn't anymore. The robots overran the place and killed everybody."

"Everybody?"

"Everybody except you, me, Rick Handel, and James. We were in the sand-crawler bay when they made their big push out, or we wouldn't have gotten out either."

Sasha whistled. "I guess I shouldn't gripe about losing an arm, then. How about what's-her-name . . . Suzi! Your little robot. Did she—?"

"Got chopped up by an ore scout on our way here."

"That's too bad. Wait a minute, Hosato. 'On our way here'? Are you trying to tell me we're at . . . ?"

She shot another glance at the uniform on the fallen guard.

". . . at Ravensteel," Hosato finished for her. "It was our only chance. I thought they might help us."

"You're nuts, Hosato. I'd rather take my chances with the robots. Ravensteel! God protect me from innocents."

"I've managed to figure it out all by myself,"

Hosato commented grimly. "Anyway, that brings us up to the present. We're trying to bust out of here before they have another chance to lavish some of their Ravensteel hospitality on us."

"Now you're talking. Where are the others?"

"Upstairs in the room above this one. I suggest it's time to regroup our forces and plan our next move."

"You know, Hosato," Sasha said, "sometimes you show a positive brilliance for tactics. Let's go. Oh, one more thing."

She wiggled her stump at him.

"They gave me some kind of stimulant to counteract the shock before they went to the truth serum. Right now I'm pillow-walking, and I don't know how long it will last or how I'll react to this arm once it wears off, so keep an eye on me, okay?"

Hosato nodded his understanding.

"Okay. Let's go."

They were halfway up the stairs when they heard the blaster fire from above.

19

Hosato bounded the rest of the way up the stairs, Sasha trailing close behind. After the initial burst of fire, the sounds from above had ceased. Weapon at the ready, Hosato slowed his pace and peered ahead at the landing.

The door to Gedge's office was open, and he could make out the smoldering form of a security guard lying in the doorway. He shot a quick glance up and down the corridor to be sure the coast was clear, then called ahead softly, "It's Hosato and Sasha! We're coming in. Hold your fire."

"All clear," James's voice came in reply.

Hosato beckoned to Sasha, and she darted across the corridor ahead of him into the office. He followed, pausing to stoop and catch the fallen guard by an armpit, dragging him inside.

"Okay," he said, shutting the door and turning to the assembled group. "Now we . . ."

He stopped suddenly as another uniformed guard appeared in the door to the adjoining room. His blaster was halfway up before he realized it was Rick.

"Hold it, Hosato!" the mechanic called, raising his hands as if to ward off an attack. "It's me."

"Right," Hosato breathed, relaxing his limbs. "Sorry. For a minute I forgot."

"I was going to ask you if you thought I could pass inspection." His friend laughed shakily. "I think you've already answered the question."

A shrill beeping from the desk-robot interrupted their tableau.

Motioning the others to silence, Hosato moved to

the desk. Taking a deep breath for relaxation, he depressed the button next to the flashing light.

"Yea?" he said into the speaker in a brisk imitation of Gedge's voice.

"Everything all right there, chief?" came a worried voice.

"Of course," Hosato barked back. "Why shouldn't it be?"

"We heard blaster fire and thought there might be trouble. Just checking to see if you needed a hand."

"One of our guests tried to go for a walk," Hosato answered jauntily. "But when the day comes I can't handle a motley bunch like this, you can have my job."

"It's a deal." The voice laughed. "But Sammy won't like it."

"That's Sammy's problem," Hosato retorted with the same joviality. "And you can tell him I said so."

There was a moment's pause before the answer came. "Right. Well, shout if you need help, chief. We'll be here waiting."

There was a brisk click as the unseen guard shut off his transmitter.

"Whew!" Rick let out his breath. "That was close."

"We may not be out of it yet," Hosato murmured thoughtfully. "Sasha, was it just me, or did our caller sound suspicious to you, too . . . there at the end?"

"It isn't just you," Sasha confirmed. "It occurs to me 'Sammy' could be a nickname for Samantha."

Hosato was kneeling at Gedge's side before she finished speaking.

"Gedge!" he snarled, shaking the injured security chief. "I don't want to have to hurt you any more. Where's the spaceport?"

"I can tell you that," Sasha supplied. "It's upstairs, directly over us."

"You're sure?"

"Come on, Hosato! Do you think we don't track their layout and security as close as they track ours?"

"Okay, let's go," Hosato said, rising. "There's probably a squad on their way here already."

"What about your gear?" James asked suddenly.

"Leave it," Hosato ordered. "I've got everything I need!"

"But your swords!" the boy insisted.

Hosato hesitated and looked at the youth's expression. For the first time he realized who had shot the guard at the door, and why.

"Okay, James," he relented. "Bring the épées . . . but that's all. We'll have to move fast."

"Say, Hosato," Sasha interrupted. "Do you still need this pig? I've waited a long time to have him in my sights."

Her blaster was pointed levelly at Gedge's head.

"Yes!" Hosato insisted more hastily than was necessary. "Rick! Bring him along. He might be our ticket out of here."

The small party traversed the stairs to the spaceport without further incident, though Hosato felt an increasing pressure for speed. He was sure that somewhere in the complex a counterattack was being prepared.

"What are you expecting to find in the spaceport?" Sasha asked.

"Hopefully a ship to get us away from this complex and off this planet," Hosato replied.

"I mean, specifically what are we going after? Do you know if there's a ship standing by for takeoff?"

"No," Hosato admitted. "We'll just have to take pot luck."

Sasha shook her head. "It doesn't work that way. They might have some company ships posted here, but it takes at least half an hour to get them ready for takeoff."

"I know that!" Hosato snapped. "If we have to take the half-hour, we'll just have to take it. I'm hoping there's something ready to go. Either way, we won't know until we check it out, will we?"

"Don't get your back up. I was just asking."

Hosato sighed. The strain of the last thirty-six hours was starting to tell on his nerves. He had catnapped in the crawler, but except for that, had had no sleep since the robot uprising.

"Sorry, Sasha. I'm just a bit tired is all."

"Shh!" came Rick's call from ahead.

Hosato hurried up the stairs to join the mechanic at the head of the formation. Rick was squatting on the stairs, a half-dozen steps short of where they terminated at a small landing. Gedge was sitting beside the mechanic, staring groggily at his shoes.

At the far side of the landing were two sets of airlocks with large glass windows in them. Through the farthest set Hosato could see a uniformed security guard apparently in casual conversation with a man in a gray jumpsuit.

"Security," Sasha hissed in his ear from close behind him. "The double doors are a safety precaution against a failure in the hookups with the ships. They can be opened only from the inside."

"That's what we have Gedge here for," Hosato replied grimly. "Rick! Get Gedge up there and rap on the glass. Don't let them see your face!"

Rick nodded his understanding. He grabbed Gedge by one arm and stood up boldly in full view of the door. Dragging his dazed charge with him, he strode to the first lock and began rapping frantically on the glass.

Surprised, the interior guard spun around and took in the scene at a glance. What he saw was one of his fellow guards supporting their chief, who was obviously in bad shape physically. Human nature took over.

The guard whirled and shoved his companion aside. He hammered two buttons in the wall panel with his fist, and the double doors opened.

"It's a trick!" Gedge managed, coming suddenly to life and trying to pull away from Rick.

The guard realized his error—too late.

Rick released Gedge and was through the door in one long bound. "Don't even twitch, sonny!" he said darkly, leveling his blaster at the startled guard.

The others swarmed through the doors after him, Hosato roughly dragging Gedge with them. Rick relieved the guard of his blaster as Sasha turned her attention to the man in the jumpsuit.

"I'll ask once," she announced. "Who or what are you?"

"I'm a . . . a taxi driver. That's all!" the man stammered. "I—I've got a ship standing by to fly some bigwigs to a conference on Theta. I'm nobody important. Really!"

Sasha laughed mirthlessly. "Nobody important. Hey, Hosato! It looks like you win. We've got a ship."

"It's about time we got lucky," Hosato growled. "Where is it?"

A shrill beeping interrupted them. A communications light was flashing on the wall panel.

"Answer it!" Rick ordered, gesturing at the guard with his blaster.

The man licked his lips nervously, then complied. "Spaceport!" he said into the speaker.

"Seal the spaceport," came a voice over the speaker. "Possible sabotage attempt in progress. They've got the chief as a hostage."

The guard's eyes darted to the group in front of him before replying. "Code Victor acknowledged."

Rick sprang forward to shove him away from the panel, but it was too late. There wasn't a member of their party that doubted the fact the guard's signal had pinpointed their location.

"That tears it," Hosato snarled. "Sasha! Is there any way they can stop our takeoff?"

"Only through the doors there," she answered briskly.

"Well, we'll just have to see how good their security

system really is. You! Where is your ship and what kind is it?"

"Pad Eight," the man responded. "It's a Starblazer III Luxury Cruiser."

"You'd better not be lying," Sasha snarled.

"It's there! So help me God! I don't want any trouble." The man seemed genuinely terror-struck.

"I can fly it," Rick volunteered.

"Okay, check it out, fast!" Hosato ordered.

"Cover him, James," Rick snapped, indicating the guard, and was gone, sprinting down the corridor.

"Gedge!" Hosato said, turning to the security chief. "I'm letting you go—"

"Wait a minute!" Sasha interrupted.

"Shut up, Sasha! Do you hear me, Gedge? I'm letting you go. The men we killed got in the way, but I don't kill people for convenience. Listen to me, Gedge! Convince those bastards about what's going on at McCrae. We weren't lying. Convince them, Gedge, or on my family's honor I'll come back here and kill you, and all the guards in the galaxy won't be able to stop me!"

"It's here!" came Rick's call from down the corridor.

"All right, get him out of here," Hosato ordered, shoving Gedge into the arms of the waiting security guard. "And move it, before I change my mind. You! The pilot! You too. Move it!"

The pilot needed no additional urging as he hastily followed the others through the doors.

Hosato slammed his hand against the door controls, and they hissed shut, sealing the spaceport against their pursuers.

"Let's get out of here," he said, starting down the corridor after Rick.

"Hosato," Sasha said, overtaking him. "Sometime we're going to have a few words about letting Gedge go."

"It's the only chance we have of convincing Raven-steel—"

They both spun at the sound of blasters behind them. The hounds were trying to burn their way through the airlocks.

"Come on, James!" Hosato urged, and the three of them sprinted for the ship.

20

"You can't count on Ravensteel to do anything," Sasha insisted. "Even if they believe Gedge, which is doubtful, they won't lift a finger. Why should they?"

Hosato sighed. This argument had been going non-stop since they lifted off from Grünbecker's Planet. He thought it was getting circular, but couldn't be sure. Lack of sleep was making his mind fuzzy.

"Look, Sasha—" he began wearily.

"Say, I hate to interrupt," Rick interrupted through the open door to the pilot's compartment, "but where are we going?"

"What was that, Rick?" Hosato blinked.

"I said, where are we going? I want to get this baby on autopilot and join the brawl. I've got a couple thoughts on the subject myself."

Hosato hadn't really given any thought to their destination. His main concern had been getting away from Grünbecker's. Still, everyone seemed to be looking at him for a decision.

"I don't know," he said, running a hand through his hair. "Pick the nearest free spaceport. We can go our separate ways from there."

"Just like that!" Sasha shouted. "Go our separate ways. Just turn our backs on the whole mess and pretend it never happened."

"What do you want us to do?" Hosato exploded. "We barely got out of there alive. If your whole security setup and guard force can't stop 'em, we sure can't."

"If we don't, who will?" She glared back.

"Hold your fire! I'm coming in!" Rick popped in

from the pilot's compartment and stood grinning at them.

"Now that I've successfully set foot in no-man's land, there are a few observations I'd like to make." He began to pace up and down the lounge, adopting the mock characteristics of a lecturer.

"First of all, Sasha's right when she says we have to do something. The robots that massacred everybody at McCrae have to be stopped, and we can't rely on anyone else to do the job. Remember, we didn't believe what was happening ourselves until it was too late and we were in the middle of it. I don't see any way anyone else is going to be convinced of the danger until it threatens them directly, and then again it will be too late."

The mechanic paused and pointed a dramatic finger at Hosato.

"On the other hand, our ace superspy here is right, too. There isn't much we can do."

"Then we're at an impasse," Hosato observed. "We have to do something, but we can't do anything. The odds are against us."

"I thought you were supposed to be some kind of expert at beating long odds," Sasha probed. "Hell, a while back you were all set to take on that same airtight security system single-handed."

"And now, between Sasha and me, you've got a ready pool of information as to what the security layout is and what makes the machines tick," Rick added.

Hosato stared at the floor. The others remained silent, letting him turn the facts over in his mind. Finally he sighed and shook his head.

"No. It still won't work." he announced. "There's one big problem no one seems ready to face. We don't know what happened back there. Until we know what went wrong, we don't know for sure what we're up against. Without that little piece of information, any plan for a counterattack would be suicidal."

The trio sat silently, each lost in their own thoughts.

"Wait a minute!" Rick exclaimed.

"What is it?" Sasha asked, but the mechanic was gone, disappearing through the door of the pilot's compartment.

He was back in a moment, brandishing a sheaf of papers in his hand.

"Do either of you speak computer?" he asked eagerly.

He dumped the papers in Hosato's lap, who bent to examine them. The papers were covered with what appeared to be typed mathematical notations interspersed with word fragments.

"What are they?" he asked.

"You should know," Rick replied smugly. "You gave 'em to me, back at the crawler bay, when you carried Sasha in."

"And you've been carrying them all this time?"

Hosato vaguely remembered the incident, but was astounded the mechanic still had the documents in his possession after all they had been through.

"Yep," Rick announced proudly. "Had 'em stashed inside my shirt. The guards who searched me at Ravensteel looked at 'em but didn't figure they were important enough to take away from me."

"For the benefit of the unenlightened," Sasha interrupted sarcastically, "what is it you've got there?"

"It's a copy of the most recent entries to the computer-monitor file," Rick informed her. "The guys were going over it at the end there, trying to figure out what went wrong and how to fix it."

"I hate to admit this," Hosato said, "but I don't know what that is or what it means."

Rick looked a bit distressed, but answered him. "Everything that's input into the central control computer passes through the monitor file . . . every program change, addition, request, everything. If we're right and Turner did something that created a new logic system in the robots, there should be a record of it here."

"I can't help you there," Sasha interjected. "What I don't know about computers could fill a library."

"Same here," Rick admitted. "I was hoping one of you . . ."

His voice trailed off as he noticed Hosato's frenzied activity. Hosato had scavenged a pencil from the depths of the bar and was busily scribbling something on the back of one of the sheets.

"Rick!" he said, handing the mechanic the paper. "Set a course for those coordinates."

"Where are we going?" Rick asked, studying the sheet.

"To visit a friend of mine," Hosato replied. "He builds and programs custom robots. Let's see if he can decipher this mess."

"Now you're talking," Rick said, brightening noticeably.

"Whoa! Don't get your hopes up yet," Hosato cautioned. "We don't know yet if he'll be able to find anything in that file. Even if he can, we've got to come up with a plan of action we all agree with, and that includes . . . say, where is James, anyway?"

Rick smiled and pointed to the back of the lounge. James was curled up on one of the luxurious sofas, fast asleep. Cradled in his arms like a teddy bear were Hosato's dueling épées.

"I think the kid has the right idea," Rick observed. "We could all do with some sleep. There are half a dozen cabins there in back. Take your pick."

"What about you?" Hosato asked.

"I'll be doing the same as soon as I get this new course fed into the autopilot." He disappeared into the pilot's compartment once more.

Hosato found himself staring at James's sleeping form.

"Leave him," Sasha said softly at his elbow. "He'll

be all right there, and he'll wake up if you try to move him."

"I guess you're right," Hosato acknowledged. "You know, Rick is quite a guy."

"Qualified to operate and repair a wide variety of heavy machinery, including space transports . . . shows a high degree of dedication when it comes to completing assignments, but displays little or no leadership ability . . . seems content in current position . . . not currently considered for advancement," Sasha recited. "You know, until all this, he was just another personnel report on my desk. Funny how you can know a person so well and not really know him at all."

"I know what you mean," Hosato admitted. "Until things blew up back there, he was just another person to pump for information. Now . . ."

His voice trailed off into silence.

"It must be a lonely way to . . ."

Sasha started to lay a hand on his arm as she spoke and succeeded only in waving her stump in the air. She stared at it for a moment, then turned away abruptly.

"Sasha . . ." Hosato said, moving to her side.

"Leave me alone!" she whispered, turning to keep her back to him.

"Sasha. It doesn't matter," he insisted.

"I don't want your pity," she snarled, and started to stalk away.

Hosato caught her before she had taken three steps.

"I'm not offering pity," he said softly. "I'm offering me. Now, if you're not interested, say so. But don't blame it on your arm."

Then she was in his arms, crying against his chest. He gently walked her down the corridor to the cabins.

21

What the Hungarian's real name was, nobody knew. He used a wide array of aliases when signing various documents, and in conversation, he responded to a variety of nicknames.

Some said he broke off a brilliant career with the corporations to start his own business; others, that the corporations stole his business away from him and he started a new one out of spite. The Hungarian had a small shop in a teeming city on a backwater planet —but his reputation was known in that part of the galaxy.

Whether he started rich or if he built his business to the point where he was wealthy was inconsequential. What mattered was the current situation, and currently he could and did pick and choose his jobs, accepting only those that were immensely expensive or particularly challenging.

Hosato had been referred to the Hungarian when searching for someone to build a fencing robot for him, and the two had become fast friends. Not that they were particularly close, for Hosato's profession did not allow confidants. Because of that, the Hungarian's stoic refusal to ask questions of a personal nature endeared him to Hosato more than anything else. As an example, they had known each other for five years after Suzi's construction was complete before Hosato had hesitantly mentioned to the Hungarian that his talents included sabotage and that he would appreciate any business that could be steered his way. When this fact was formally mentioned, the Hungarian immediately produced not one, but three clients for Hosato. Apparently he had had his suspicions all along, probably from the "special construction" that went into Suzi, but had refrained from seeking clarification or confirmation until Hosato broached the subject himself.

Hosato was reluctant to face him with the news of Suzi's demise, but he needn't have worried. The Hungarian greeted them upon their arrival with his usual expansive welcome and was introduced to Sasha, Rick, and James without once commenting on Suzi's absence. In fact, the subject was not even broached until later over drinks, after they had briefed the Hungarian on the events at McCrae and the problem at hand.

When they had finished their tale, he sat silently puffing on his pipe for several minutes before responding.

"You know, Hosato," he said at last, "if you hadn't brought along a brace of witnesses for your yarn, I'd think this was all an elaborate excuse for losing one of the best robots I've ever built."

"I know it sounds impossible—" Sasha began.

The Hungarian waved a hand of dismissal at her. "When you've worked with machines as long as I have," he declared, "you learn nothing is impossible —highly improbable, perhaps, but not impossible."

"Can you read these?" Rick asked, eagerly producing his sheaf of papers. "It's a copy of the last entries to the central Computer-Monitor file," the mechanic announced proudly. "We were hoping you might be able to tell from these what went wrong."

"Not so fast." The Hungarian exhaled a long stream of pipe smoke. "It's too soon for detail. Let's approach this problem one step at a time. First of all, what is the basic problem?"

"Come on, Tinker," Hosato groaned. "The problem is that robots are killing people."

"Wrong." The Hungarian pointed his pipe stem at Hosato. "The problem is that the McCrae complex is

producing robots that are killing people. That makes
it a problem with the computer, and not a malfunctioning of the robots themselves."

"That's right," Rick asserted. "We think something
went wrong with the programming when Turner,
James's father, was trying to design a new security-
robot system. Probably something that bypassed the
'no-kill' base programming."

The Hungarian shook his head. "It's not that simple. We're talking about an 'activity program.' That
means, in addition to capacity, it needs motivation."

It was clear that the Hungarian had risen to the
bait and was rapidly becoming enmeshed in what to
him was a puzzle of electronics and computer logic.
Hosato was glad to see him involved, though the conversation rapidly became too complex and technical
for laymen such as himself to follow.

When James got up and wandered off into the small
kitchen and no one noticed, Hosato decided to follow
suit. The other three were huddled over the monitor
log copies and didn't even look up as he left.

James was pouring himself a glass of pop and
looked up as Hosato joined him. He brightened noticeably.

"Could you pour two more of those while you're
at it?" Hosato asked.

"Sure. No problem."

As the boy hurried about his errand, Hosato pondered the best way to approach the subject on his
mind.

"Say, James," he said at last. "We haven't had
much time to talk since the blowup at McCrae."

"Talk about what?" James asked, passing his friend
the glass of soft drink and perching on the counter.

"About your future, mostly," Hosato responded
pointedly.

"I thought that was all settled," James replied inno-
cently. "I'm going with you."

"It's not that simple, and you know it. Look,

James," Hosato began. "You don't know anything about me or how I live. Now, I don't know what kind of romantic notion you have in your head about the kind of person I am, but it's not a life-style you enter into casually."

"I'm not doing this casually," James protested. "I asked you to take me along with you before things went bad at the complex . . . before Dad was killed, too. Besides, I don't have anywhere else to go."

"That's what I mean!" Hosato pounced on the phrase.

Without realizing it, he began to pace back and forth in the cramped kitchen.

"James, there are lots of things you could do. You're bright. You're energetic. You've got guts. And you've got a whole lot of options before you. Don't be stampeded into any one life just because you feel there's no other choice. . . . Particularly my kind of life. Now I don't mean to sound negative on all this, but I've been traveling the star lanes most of my life and I've seen this time and time again. Men and women working at jobs they hate, their whole lives just a drone existence, all with the same story, 'I didn't have any other choice.' Well, by God, you do have choices. Life should be a series of choices. Some lock you in, a few lock you out, and then there are others that open more doors. Making good choices demands brains, some luck, and a whole lot of guts. And most of all, it takes that something that makes us human . . . the will to make ourselves better. James, don't lock yourself into the first chance that you get. And that's what this life will do. Don't be looking back ten or fifteen years past the star lanes wishing you hadn't committed to something you can't get out of. James, don't make choices like a programmed robot!"

Hosato stopped, realizing how emotional he was becoming.

"Is that why you said no the first time I asked you?" the boy prompted.

"That's right. I'll tell you now, I was tempted to go along with it even then. My work is lonely. To give you an idea how lonely, Suzi was my best friend until she was destroyed, covering our retreat. Do you understand what I'm saying? My best friend was a robot. That should give you an idea of how low things can get."

"I liked Suzi," James protested.

Hosato ignored him. "You've got a dozen ways you could go with your life. I'm only one of them. At this moment, I just happen to be the closest option to you. I can't let you make your decision on that basis." Then with a quick wink, an attempt to lighten the conversation, he added, "Listen kid, I've got my own dubious concept of honor, you know."

"How did you get into this business?" James asked pointedly.

Hosato was silent for a few moments, then leaned against the counter as he answered.

"That's a good question, James, and it deserves an honest answer. With me, I really didn't have a choice, or rather, the choice was made for me. It's a family business, and I was raised into it. For me, it's as natural as breathing. For many reasons, I couldn't leave it now if I wanted to. But I'll tell you this much, James, I'm not particularly happy with what I do. Sometimes I wonder, if I were starting all over again and given a choice, and I knew what I know now, if I wouldn't walk away from it all without looking back. You've got that choice, and I want you to think it through before commiting yourself."

James bit his lip thoughtfully. "All right, Hosato," he said. "Tell me about this terrible life. What *do* you do?"

Now it was Hosato's turn to lapse into silence. Waves of bitter memories held in check by sheer force of will now flooded over him. He had set himself up for this question; now he had to answer it, both for the boy and for himself.

"I'm a killing machine," he said quietly. "I kill people. Not because they're a threat or even because they may have offended me—not that that's a good reason. I kill because I'm paid to."

He fixed James with a calm gaze as he continued.

"You want to know what it means to be in my line of work? I said you don't have any friends. Well, that was a lie. You have lots of friends. But your profession makes a mockery of the word 'friendship.' You worm your way into people's confidence, and when they trust you implicitly, you destroy them. Rick's my friend. We used to drink together back at McCrae. All the time we were together, I was getting information to shut the complex down. At the very least, it would have put him out of work—permanently, if anyone ever found out he was a security leak. If he had found out what I was about or surprised me while I was working, I would have killed him."

He deliberately let his voice harden. "You remember what it's like to kill people, don't you?"

James's gaze wavered and dropped to the floor.

Hosato fought and conquered an urge to console the boy. He waited in silence while the boy relived his first blooding.

"Hosato," James said at last, not lifting his gaze, "I don't know about the killing. Back at Ravensteel, when I killed those men . . . I don't know. I'm glad I saved our lives, that I was good enough with weapons to do it, but I still feel a little sick when I think about it!"

"Are you proud?" Hosato asked.

"What?" James raised his eyes at last.

"Are you proud of killing two men? If you get a chance, are you going to brag about it to the Hungarian?"

The boy hesitated, then dropped his gaze once more and shook his head. "No," he said softly. "They were just enemies I killed. They weren't people, I guess. They were just enemies."

"Look at me, James," Hosato demanded. He fixed his eyes deep into James. "They were people you killed. They weren't robots that you terminated. They were two human beings, lives with loved ones, lives with dreams—people capable of wonderful things, as well, of course, as killing you. They weren't just enemies, they were human beings."

Hosato slid an arm around the boy's shoulders. "James," he said. "Let me tell you what my grandfather told me, the same grandfather who trained me for this work. He said, 'You must learn to kill because it is necessary. To be effective, you must kill coldly and without hesitation. But killing is not to be taken lightly nor is it to be taken pridefully. Kill as well, as skillfully as you can, knowing that killing is man's fatal flaw.'

"That's good advice, James. Listen to it."

They both turned, to find Sasha framed in the door.

"Sorry to interrupt," she said, "but I think we've got something out here."

Hosato clapped James lightly on the back. "Think about what I've said. There's no rush. Now, go on ahead. There's something I want to say to Sasha."

The boy's eyes darted between the two of them, and he smiled.

"Okay, Hosato," he said, vaulting down off the counter. "I'll tell them you'll be there in a minute."

"The kid looks like he'll pull through this okay," Sasha commented, watching James's departure.

"Sasha," Hosato began, "we've got to talk."

"No," she said firmly. "It's pointless to talk about the future until we know for sure if we've got one. Now, come on and join the group. This is important."

She was gone before Hosato could reply, leaving him no choice but to follow her back into the other room.

"There you are!" the Hungarian called. "For a world-saver, you spend a lot of time goofing off."

"What have you got?" Hosato asked, ignoring the jibe.

"Well," the Hungarian said, leisurely lighting his pipe, "the problem is that Turner didn't think things through. That's always a mistake. There's always the temptation to let the computers do our thinking for us because they do it so much faster. It's quicker to rough out an idea and let the machines develop it, then fine-tune it until it does what we want."

Hosato writhed with impatience, but knew from experience it was useless to try to rush the Hungarian.

"That's what Turner did, and learned the hard way the price of turning development over to machines. They think fast, too fast. Any mistake that's made is carried out before you can correct your input, and Turner made a beaut."

"Which was . . . ?" Hosato prompted.

"He changed the 'no-kill' program. Now, he wasn't completely stupid. He gave the computer specific parameters. He gave it the capacity to kill, to defend itself . . . if the computer or the manufacturing units were threatened."

"What's wrong with that?" James asked.

"Two things," the Hungarian replied. "First of all, he didn't define completely what constituted a threat, so the computer came up with its own definition."

"So when Turner tried to shut down the operation, the computer interpreted it as a threat and had the prototypes kill him!" Sasha completed the thought with sudden awareness.

"Exactly." The Hungarian beamed.

"That can't be all of it, Tinker," Hosato insisted. "I wasn't directly threatening the operation when the robots took their first two tries at me . . . and certainly the families in the living mall weren't a threat. What happened there?"

"That's Turner's second mistake," the Hungarian announced, relighting his pipe. "Actually, it involves a completely different command, way back at the beginning of the project. Apparently Turner was afraid of anyone else stealing his idea, so he did two things. First, he put a voice lock on his program terminal. Second, he instructed the computer to keep the project secret from anyone who did not enter the program from his terminal. He was very explicit, instructing the computer to guard the secret with every power at its disposal."

"How was it supposed to do that?" Hosato asked.

"By giving meaningless or misdirecting information when asked," Sasha informed him. "It's a very bright computer and can be incredibly evasive when it wants. What I don't understand is how that affects things. Most of the line managers put in secret preserving instructions when they start a new project. They're paranoid that way. What makes Turner's instructions any different?"

"You're right, Sasha," the Hungarian agreed. "By itself it's quite innocent. The trouble comes when you add his later order giving the computer a kill capacity. Now killing is within its power, and it is to do everything in its power to preserve Turner's secret. See the problem?"

"Oh, my God!" Sasha gasped as the enormity of the situation dawned on her.

The group sat in stunned silence. Only the Hungarian seemed unperturbed, puffing on his pipe as he continued.

"Actually, Hosato, there's a good chance you triggered all this. It might have been better if the machines had killed you."

"Wait a minute—" Hosato began, but the Hungarian waved him back to silence.

"I was merely pointing out that when you escaped from the manufacturing area, you signed the death warrant for everyone in the McCrae complex. The computer couldn't be sure whom you had talked to, so to preserve Turner's secret, it simply killed everyone."

"Now, don't try to hang this on Hosato!" Sasha

intervened. "He didn't program the damn computer. Besides, all of us here got away from the robots, not just Hosato."

"True enough," the Hungarian acknowledged. "But that was to survive the attack triggered by Hosato's earlier escape. However, that does raise an interesting problem. If I'm correct, the robots massacred the humans at the McCrae complex to eliminate any information leak Hosato might have caused. Now, four of you escaped from the massacre. Extending the same logic . . ."

". . . those things will try to kill every human in the universe," Rick said softly. "All to preserve Turner's bloody secret project. Mother of God!"

Hosato barely noticed the exchange. His mind was already turning over plans for a counterattack, analyzing them and gauging their strengths and weaknesses. Whether or not mankind as a whole was being threatened was inconsequential. He had indirectly been the cause of the death of several hundred innocent people. He was now honor-bound to destroy the murderers, to avenge those innocent deaths, even if his own life was sacrificed in the effort.

ഛഛഛഛഛഛഛഛ **22** ഛഛഛഛഛഛഛഛ

To the Hungarian fell the lot of traveling to Grünbecker's Planet on a preliminary scouting mission. The others hadn't liked it, but he successfully defended his suggestion. None could challenge his qualifications as a scout in this situation. Perhaps most convincing was his argument that of the five of them, he was the only one whose descriptive stats weren't in the McCrae personnel-data files.

His plan was simple enough—to join one of the tour groups visiting McCrae Enterprises and make his observations in the safe disguise of a tourist. It was agreed that the planning of their counterattack would wait until his return, both for the data he would bring and for his expert counsel.

In the interim, the weary refugees were forced to find activities to occupy their leisure time. Rick found refuge in the Hungarian's extensive library, losing himself for hours in the stacks of text to the point that he frequently failed to appear for meals. Sasha enlisted James's aid and took advantage of the Hungarian's small gymnasium and firing range. It was still her intent to participate in the final assault on McCrae, and to that end drilled herself mercilessly to adjust to the loss of her right arm. She firmly rejected Hosato's offers of assistance, preferring to practice alone or with James as a companion.

Left to his own devices, Hosato made use of the workshop to check and prepare what was left of his equipment. It soon became apparent to him, however, that he was in actuality stalling—avoiding a duty he was reluctant to fulfill.

Finally, however, he could no longer ignore his conscience and reluctantly locked himself in the Hungarian's communications room.

It took a while to establish contact, which was not surprising, as long-range communications equipment was not common on Musashi, but after many relays and delays he was confronted with the holographic image of his grandfather. The figure of the elder Hosato, elegant in a simple black kimono, appeared floating inches off the floor in a seated position. That, coupled with the fact his eyes focused at a point several feet behind Hosato, indicated the transmission/receiving gear was not adjusted properly. Still, it was an incredible technical feat to have the image this clear, considering the distances involved.

The figure motioned to Hosato, indicating a place in the air directly in front of it. Hosato responded, kneeling on the floor, his hands resting on his thighs.

"You are looking well, my son," the image said. The voice was strong and reverberant.

"And you, grandfather," Hosato replied.

He was genuinely relieved to see his grandfather in such good health. The elder Hosato was in his nineties but he sat ramrod straight. His tight unlined face rested on a sinewy pillar of a throat that loomed up from muscular shoulders. It had been five years since Hosato had last spoken to him directly.

"Your mother and sister have been worried about you," the image continued. "It has been many years since we have heard from you."

"I apologize for any distress I might have caused them. Since leaving home, I have traveled far, and on the occasions I could afford to communicate with you, proper facilities were not available."

"We are not wealthy," his grandfather pointed out sternly. "But we would have accepted the expense of such a communication to hear from our eldest son."

Hosato hung his head. "Though I knew this, my

pride would not let me impose such a burden on you. Forgive me."

The image waved a ghostly hand. "Enough of such talk," it said. "Tell me of your adventures since you left us."

"Most recently, I had a supporting role in a production of *Down the Alley* on Tansil," Hosato responded.

"I am not familiar with this play," the image stated.

"It is a very old script. The story revolves around a young criminal who . . ."

To a casual observer viewing the conversation, it would seem to be a normal, though prolonged, exchange of pleasantries, gossip, and news between father and son.

It wasn't.

The Hosato family, true Ninjas that they were, were very close with their secrets. They did not engage in idle conversation. The fact that Hosato contacted his family at all was an immediate indication that he was facing a crisis, one that either required the family's counsel or was a direct threat to the family.

As they spoke, Hosato and the image of his grandfather, their hands and fingers moved minutely, constantly changing position. It was not the hand signals of the deaf-mutes or the sign language of the Great Plains Indians. It was the Hosato family code, which had been passed along for generations. It was drilled into all members of the family until they were able to carry on two conversations simultaneously, one verbal, which served only to cover the real conversation passing between the subtly moving hands. Many people spoke Japanese, but only the family knew this code.

After Hosato's hands had finished explaining the current situation, his grandfather immediately formed the question he had been dreading.

"What of your companions?" the fingers asked.

"I seek advice on how to proceed with my mission,"

Hosato countered. "I am faced with a foe that threatens the existence of mankind."

"Mankind has faced many threats," came the reply from the image's hands. "Yet it still survives. Your companions constitute a direct threat to our family."

"The mechanic does not possess sufficient knowledge of our activities to constitute a threat," he explained.

"And the woman and the boy?"

There it was. His grandfather had now asked the question directly. Hosato could no longer evade the issue.

"I was considering sponsoring them into the family," he stated.

The image's hands were motionless for several moments before replying.

"A family member may sponsor only one outsider for membership." The fingers formed the words with a crisp abruptness. "It is the law."

"I was hoping that under the circumstances, an exception could be made to the law," Hosato appealed.

"It is the law," came the firm answer.

"As current head of the family, it is within your power to change or modify the law," Hosato pleaded.

"My son," the image responded slowly, "the laws of the family are not to be changed lightly. Perhaps if you live to succeed me as head of the family, you will realize that."

"I do not ask lightly now!" Hosato insisted. "I only ask—"

"You ask me to change one of the oldest laws of the family," the image interrupted. "To save you from having to make a difficult decision. I will not."

Hosato experienced a sinking sensation in his stomach as the image's fingers continued their statement.

"There are two outsiders who now possess enough information about our family to pose a threat to its continued existence. You may sponsor only one for membership. The other must be eliminated. As you were the source of their information, it becomes your task to carry out the mission. Fail in this, and you will no longer be considered a member of the family. We will speak no more of this."

"My grandfather," Hosato motioned desperately, "I would ask that you keep an open mind on this. You yourself have said the strength of a law is in its flexibility."

"As to your mechanical foes"—the image continued ignoring him—"if you insist on involving yourself further in this affair, remember your training. If faced by an enemy possessing superior strength and speed, seek a way to use that strength and speed to your advantage. Do not directly oppose, but yield and add your own strength and speed to that of your enemy to create a force greater than that directed against you."

Hosato paid only partial attention to the image's advice. The rest of his concentration was focused on the problem confronting him. His grandfather would not reconsider or even hear additional arguments on the subject of Sasha and James. He simply dictated that one of them must die, then dismissed the matter.

"I shall remember your advice, my grandfather," Hosato signaled.

"Do you have any further questions or need for counsel?" the fingers asked.

Hosato thought for a moment.

"How many members of the family have been excommunicated in the past?" he asked finally.

There was a pause before the image's hands moved in answer.

"I do not know," it said. "If a member is so banished, all references and records of him are stricken from the family history."

Hosato thought for a moment more.

"I have no further questions," he signaled at last.

"I fear our time for conversation draws to an end my son," the image said, returning to the verbal line of communication. "You must contact us more often, neh? In the meantime, continue to conduct yourself in a manner your family can take pride in. *Sayonara.*"

"I will remember, my grandfather. *Sayonara* and *domo!*" Hosato replied, and watched as the image faded to nothingness.

He remained motionless for long minutes after contact was broken, lost in thought.

Could he do it? Could he coldly kill either Sasha or James to preserve the curtain of secrecy around the Hosato family? Or should he openly defy his father, and in doing so face banishment from his family?

He tried to weigh the consequences of each action in his mind, but they merged and ran together in a confused kaleidoscope of indecision.

Shimatta! He had made a mistake—a big one. The only question in his mind was whether the mistake was taking James and Sasha into his confidence or in seeking his grandfather's advice and approval.

Finally he shook his head. Perhaps Sasha was right. It was foolish to consider the future until it was known if there would be a future. There was every probability the upcoming mission against the McCrae robots would solve the problem for him. If not, he could make his decision then.

He rose and went to join the others.

23

"That's some complex!" the Hungarian stated enthusiastically to the group, once they had reconvened. "Do you think someday my little workshop here will grow up to be like that?"

Hosato was in no mood for humorous banter. "Come on," he interrupted. "We've been waiting for your report."

The Hungarian waved his drink at him. "And you can't wait another five minutes? Not even for a few social pleasantries?" he protested. "I've been back only fifteen minutes, and you—"

"Please . . . ?" Sasha asked gently.

"The impatience of youth!" The Hungarian sighed. "Very well, my dear. For *you*, I'll start."

For effect, he paused to light his pipe, his eyes dancing mischievously at Hosato's impatient fidgeting.

"First off," he began finally, "I wasn't rushing my report, because I don't have that much to add. As might be suspected from the Ravensteel reaction, tour groups are still being processed through McCrae without any noticeable change. There are no humans in sight, but it's my understanding there never were on these tours. Everything is functioning normally, and if I didn't trust you all implicitly, I'd swear nothing such as you described ever took place at the complex."

He paused to relight his pipe.

"Believe me, Tinker—" Hosato began.

The Hungarian silenced him with a vague wave.

"I believe, I believe!" he said. "I was talking about what the normal eye would see. Fortunately, I have

186

better-than-normal eyes. You know those cameras and sensors you told me to watch for?"

He cocked an eyebrow at Sasha, who nodded.

"Well, they've been embellished. They each have new little doodads attached. I couldn't tell for sure what they were without close examination, but I have a strong feeling they aren't room deodorizers."

"Blasters?" Hosato asked.

The Hungarian shrugged. "Like I say, I couldn't tell without close examination, and somehow I didn't think it would be wise to attempt it. Then for laughs I tried the Employment Office and was politely informed by the desk-robot there were no positions available at this time."

The group sat in silence for several long minutes digesting what they had heard, each lost in his own thoughts.

"Okay," Hosato said at last, "Rick and Sasha have put together floor plans and schematics as to what we're up against at the McCrae complex. What's your appraisal of the situation?"

The Hungarian blew a long plume of smoke from his pipe before replying.

"You're facing a highly automated manufacturing complex with multiple security devices. Unlike normal electronic detection devices, these are armed and it is assumed they will fire on any detected threat to the complex. In addition, there is an unknown number of mobile robots guarding the complex against intrusion, also armed. The key to the whole mess is here."

He paused to tap the indicated spot on the layout drawings with the stem of his pipe.

"The Central Computer Building. The computer housed here controls the entire operation; the security scanners, the mobile killer modules, and the manufacturing concern producing the killer modules. Correct its programming or destroy it completely, and the whole complex goes down."

"Wait a minute," Hosato interrupted. "Back up a

little. Did you say we could stop the computer by correcting its programming?"

"That's right."

"Then that's what we'll do! It's got to be easier than getting to the computer itself."

The Hungarian shook his head. "Not so fast. We can't use just any terminal to change the programming. Tell him, Sasha."

"There are lots of terminals, Hosato, but only a handful that give you access to the program banks," the former security chief informed him. "What's more, it seems one of Turner's precautions was to lock out the other program terminals. The only one we could use is the one in his office."

Hosato pulled the layout map toward him and scanned it to refresh his memory.

"That's still our best bet," he declared. "Compared to the route to the computer building, reaching Turner's office is the yellow brick road."

"No it isn't," Sasha corrected. "The terminal in Turner's office won't help us at all."

"But you said—"

"I said it was the only terminal that could change the base programs. Unfortunately, we can't use it."

"Why not?" Hosato asked.

"Because of the idiot voice lock he has on it," she snarled. "I was fighting him through channels trying to get it removed for security reasons when this mess blew up. Now he's dead and there's no way we can bypass the lock."

Hosato experienced a moment of frustration; then he quelled it. With effort he forced himself to abandon the hope of using the terminal and concentrate on the Central Computer Building. If that was where they would have to attack, that was that. Railing against facts didn't change them.

The others waited in silence as he pored over the floor plans, respectful of an expert at work. Time and time again he checked a measurement or an angle, then shook his head.

"I'll have to think on this overnight," he announced at last. "There's *got* to be a way."

"Any ideas at all?" Rick asked.

Hosato shook his head. "Frankly, right now it looks impossible. I can't see any way two people can crack that layout."

"Two?" Sasha queried.

In response, Hosato cocked an eyebrow at the Hungarian, who cleared his throat uncomfortably.

"What your friend here is trying to say, Sasha, is that you shouldn't count on me for a fight," he said. "You're welcome to whatever equipment or weapons I can supply, and I'll advise you as best I can, but I'm simply not a man of action. I'm sorry if you think less of me for that, but that's the way I am. When the actual mission starts, I'm a cheering section and not much more."

"That's all right," Sasha assured him. "You've been more than enough help already."

"Say . . . um . . . Hosato," Rick interjected. "Maybe this isn't the time to bring it up, but Sasha and I have been talking, and . . ."

"Yes?" Hosato prompted.

"Well, we think that she should go along with you on this mission. Even with her . . . disability . . . she can shoot better than I can, and—"

"—and she can't pilot a ship, while you can," Hosato finished for him. "I know. I've been figuring 'all along that Sasha would be my backup."

The Hungarian shot him a look of surprise and suspicion. Hosato ignored it and continued.

"That's why I'm trying to come up with a plan for two. The Hungarian stays here, and you pilot the ship, which leaves Sasha and me for the assault. By my count, that's two."

"Three," said James, breaking his silence. "I'm going too."

"James—" Hosato began.

"I'm going," the boy said firmly. "My father started all this, and I'm going to help finish it. Besides, I can beat the voice lock."

"What?" Sasha exploded into life.

"I said, I can beat the voice lock," James stated calmly. "It's keyed to open for either of two voices. One was Dad's, the other's mine."

"Sasha, can we use a recording of his voice to do the job?" Hosato asked.

"No," the boy answered. "The lock involves a series of three random questions that have to be answered within a given time span. It was designed that way to prevent someone using a recorded voice to force the lock."

Sasha looked at the Hungarian. "Could you teach him what to say to change the program once he springs the lock?"

He sighed. "I could try, but it's a lot to teach him in two weeks."

"Why 'two weeks'?" Rick interrupted.

The Hungarian slapped his forehead in mock astonishment.

"That's just like me!" he announced viciously. "Here I've been worrying about it all the way back here, and then I forget to show you."

He rummaged in his pocket for a moment and fished out a folded piece of paper.

"Here," he said, passing it to Rick. "Read this. McCrae Enterprises is announcing its revolutionary new line of security robots. According to that release, demonstrator sets will be available for shipment to interested customers within three weeks."

"And it will take us a week just to get there," Rick moaned. "Hosato . . ."

He stopped. Hosato was sitting with the layout maps in his hands, a vague smile on his face.

"What is it?" Rick asked.

"I believe the man has a plan," the Hungarian observed.

"You're right." Hosato smiled. "Just an outline right now, but I think the details can be worked out. Sasha, you and James are going in with a tour group. Once you're in the complex, you get to Turner's office, activate the terminal, and change the program."

"And what will you be doing in the meantime?" the former security chief asked archly.

"Me?" Hosato's smile broadened. "I'll be creating a diversion."

24

Hosato watched the Ravensteel robots from his chosen place of concealment in a cluster of boulders up the slope from the ore vein. For nearly five hours now he had sat motionless, studying the machines as they labored at their task.

Below him the giant machines gouged and sliced monstrous hunks of ore from the exposed vein, lifting them into the waiting transport machines. As each transport in its turn was filled, it turned and began its trek back to the Ravensteel complex, another lurching forward to take its place at the fill point.

From his vantage point Hosato could see the long, broken line of transports trundling over the horizon, and its sister line of transports returning empty for another load.

"The tour ship is approaching," Rick's voice came in his ear.

"Acknowledged," Hosato replied.

The Hungarian had been true to his word. Though not accompanying them, he had been more than generous in providing them with equipment. The surface suit Hosato was currently wearing was a vast improvement over the bulky affair he had tried to don in the McCrae sand crawler. Its built-in communications system allowed him to maintain constant contact with Rick, waiting in the ship, while its close fit allowed him a freedom of movement he would not have believed possible in a surface suit. Most important, he could wear his invisibility suit over it.

Having received Rick's signal, Hosato broke the

seal of his Ninja suit. For this job, he wanted to be
seen.

On the ground beside him were two tripod-mounted
rifle blasters, more gifts from the Hungarian. Hosato
picked one up and carefully eased it forward. The
robots were still rumbling about their programmed
tasks, unaware of his presence as he chose his first
target and settled the cross hairs of his weapon on it.

He gently depressed the two firing lugs, and the
weapon responded, a pencil-thin beam of energy darting forth, momentarily locking marksman and target
together. At the other end of the beam, his target robot, the one farthest away of those visible to him,
ground to a sudden halt.

Hosato waited several seconds, then triggered the
weapon twice more in rapid succession. His second
target, a robot at the ore face, imitated the first, jolt-
ing to rigid immobility. The third, loading a large
chunk of ore onto a transport, went amok. Lurching
forward, it rolled over the waiting transport unit,
crushing it like a toy, and headed blindly into a rock
formation. There, its forward momentum stopped, it
began to slowly dig itself into the side of the abutment.

Hosato did not pause to watch the results of his
marksmanship. He was busy firing sporadically but
carefully into the robots below him. Then he rose and
stepped from his hiding place, standing boldly in the
open as he surveyed his handiwork.

Hosato smiled at the carnage. Nearly fifty robots
had been seriously disabled or destroyed by his assault. About half a dozen robots still partially func-
tioned. To be specific, though their movement might
be impaired, their internal units that maintained communications with the central coordinating computer
back at the Ravensteel complex were still fully active,
as were their camera units. He had listened well when
Rick outlined the operational modules of ore robots
and their internal arrangement.

Terribly sloppy, instigating an attack and then failing to complete the carnage, particularly failing to break the enemy's communication chain. It's just the sort of blunder you would expect from a professional security guard suddenly assigned to play soldier.

There was even one fully operational robot down there. It was currently sitting far back in a shadowy ravine watching him. He couldn't see it, but he had noted its retreat and deliberately allowed it to occur.

Aside from ensuring that data of his appearance would be relayed to Ravensteel, it was a good sign. The robot's self-preserving maneuver, a clear break in pattern from its normal mining activity, indicated that someone or something at Ravensteel was feeding it new instructions. Whether it was the central co-ordinating computer or one of its human monitors did not matter. His attack had been noted, and counter-measures were already underway.

Smiling, he turned and headed over the crest of the ridge toward his rendezvous with the ship and with Rick. Mission accomplished! Ravensteel had experienced an attack on their operations by an obviously hostile force. Now, who on Grünbecker's Planet would qualify as a hostile force? When the retaliation strike came, whom would it be directed against?

Hosato's smile broadened. The robots at McCrae were about to experience a diversionary attack that would be impossible to ignore.

"Still nothing?" Hosato asked anxiously, peering over Rick's shoulder at the bank of instruments.

He was totally unfamiliar with the sensor system and ignorant of how to read the dials and wave patterns, but the action gave him a much-needed activity.

"If there was, I'd tell you!" Rick snapped. "Now, will you quit asking me the same question every thirty seconds?"

"I don't understand it," Hosato said, shaking his head. "They should have done *something* by now."

Their ship was concealed a short distance from the McCrae complex. Inside, the two men waited to monitor the Ravensteel counterattack, an attack that had failed to develop.

"Maybe they recognized you," Rick suggested. "Sasha and I both told you it was a mistake to leave Gedge alive."

"And all of us agreed that if I were recognized, they'd assume I was acting under orders from Mc-Crae," Hosato retorted. "Either way, it adds up to McCrae as the target for their retaliation."

"I bet they went after the McCrae ore robots," Rick said firmly. "Punishment equal to the crime or some such. 'They hit our miners, we hit their miners!' Just because they come after McCrae doesn't mean they'll attack the main complex."

"If they hit the ore robots, they're in for a rude surprise," Hosato said grimly. "McCrae robots shoot back. When the humans of Ravensteel get fired on by robots, they'll have to believe our story. Once our 'killer-robot' report is accepted, Ravensteel has to attack the complex just out of self-preservation."

"But will they do it today?" Rick argued. "Corporations take forever to make decisions, and even longer to act on them. That's assuming, of course, they get the report at all. What happens if no one survives the attack on the ore robots?"

Hosato made his decision.

"You're right, Rick. There are too many variables. Too many ifs. I should have seen it in the plan. I'm just not used to working with a team!"

"Come on, Hosato, take it easy," Rick said soothingly. "There's nothing we can do now."

"That's where you're wrong, Rick. There's something I can do, and I'm going to do it. I'm going in myself."

Rick was openly taken aback at the idea.

"You're nuts!" he declared. "We've gone over it a

hundred times. It's suicide for you to go in there alone."

"The tour group's in there already, right?" Hosato pressed. "Sasha and James are waiting for a diversion. You know Sasha. Do you think she'll back away from it just because the attack doesn't come? If it's suicide for me to go in there armed and with all my equipment, what chance do the two of them have? A boy and a one-armed woman? Against the whole security network?"

"I hate to put a damper on heroic gestures, Hosato," Rick said carefully. "But what difference does it make if you go or not . . . except getting three people killed instead of two?"

"The difference"—Hosato sighed—"is that if I go, there's still a chance—not much, but still a chance— that we can stop this mess before it spreads. If it gets off Grünbecker's, nobody will be able to stop it.".

25

"Rick!"

"Yes, Hosato?"

The mechanic's voice came clearly through his suit communicator.

"Did you close the bay doors behind us when we escaped in the sand crawler?"

There was a long pause before the answer came.

"I can't remember. I think I did, but I couldn't say for sure. That whole day is a bit of a blur. Why?"

"Just wondered."

Hosato contemplated the doors leading to the sand-crawler bay. The inner and outer doors of the airlock were standing wide open. Inside, he could see the interior of the sand-crawler bay, apparently unchanged from when they had so hastily left in their escape from the robots. It looked innocent enough, but Hosato felt a nagging of suspicion as he studied the entrance.

Like Rick, he thought they had closed the doors behind them, but couldn't be sure. The gaping portals looked uncomfortably like the yawning jaws of a trap.

Well, he'd come to create a diversion. Still, if he was successfully ambushed upon entering the complex, there would be no need to draw other robots away from Sasha and James's target area. Sealing his invisibility suit as a precaution, he eased his way through the doors and entered the complex.

There were no robots in the crawler bay. In fact, there was no indication they had even penetrated to this point. The second sand crawler was still standing in its partially assembled state, as Rick left it, and the door to the maintenance shop was closed.

Hosato manually closed and sealed the inner airlock door. To activate the machinery would immediately alert the computer to his presence, as would opening the door to the maintenance shop without first closing the airlock. He wanted to penetrate a bit deeper into the complex before beginning his diversion.

He had to steel himself to open the door to the maintenance shop. Though a death merchant by profession, he did not relish viewing the aftermath of the robots' massacre of the McCrae humans.

He needn't have worried.

When he finally eased the door open, an astounding sight greeted his eyes. There was no sign of the massacre at all! There were no bodies, no bloodstains or disorder, no visual evidence of a struggle at all. The shop stood vacant and immaculate, as if the humans had merely stepped out for a moment.

No, not quite. Adjusting to the shock, Hosato studied the room more carefully and could now detect the signs of the robots' handiwork. It was too perfect, too neat. Humans would never maintain a workshop in this immaculate condition. This looked more like a display from an equipment showroom than a well-used workshop.

Casting about, his eye settled on a waist-high workstool mounted on swivel wheels. Yes, that would do fine. Working one-handed, he moved two heavy tool boxes onto the stool seat. He was loath to set his hand blaster down, even for the barest second. It was his only weapon and he didn't want to be surprised by a security robot without having it in his hand.

Pushing the now-laden workstool in front of him, he moved to the side door, the one that opened into the corridor leading to the Central Computer Building. Cautiously he opened the door and eased his head inside.

The corridor was clear. The robots he had destroyed

on the day of their escape had been removed. That made more sense than the removal of the human bodies. Robot parts could be reused.

Taking a deep breath, he broke the seal of his suit, allowing himself to become visible for the first time since entering the complex. It was time to start his diversion.

Dragging the workstool behind him, he moved slowly down the corridor. There should not be any security devices until he reached the first intersection, but they had no way of knowing what new traps the robots may have installed during their absence.

His caution proved unnecessary. He arrived at the first intersection without any new devices registering on his sensors. A short corridor came into his corridor at this point, forming a T. He would have to traverse this connecting corridor, but the drawings he had studied at the Hungarian's indicated a trap at the midway point. It was designed as an alarm trigger only, but again the robots might have modified it since.

Easing the workstool around in front of him, he gave it a vigorous shove, sending it rolling into the alarm zone.

Nothing happened.

Hosato watched with growing suspicion as the stool rolled on unhindered, until it crashed into the far wall, one of the toolboxes clattering to the floor with the impact.

Strange. Perhaps the stool had not been heavy enough to trigger the alarm.

He swept the corridor with his sensors. There was no reading on the watch dial. The zone was inoperative! Could Sasha and James have been successful so soon?

As if in answer to his question, there came a sound from the corridor behind him, the sound of a robot approaching. Reflexively Hosato flattened against the wall, his blaster ready.

Now. Now it starts.

He waited until the sounds were closer, then stepped around the corner, his weapon leveled. As his eyes took in the figure in the corridor, his fingers froze on the firing lugs. It was . . .

"Suzi!" he exclaimed.

"There is no time to lose," Suzi replied briskly. "Follow me—quickly!"

The robot spun about and started back down the corridor.

A thousand questions flashed through Hosato's mind. Then he forced his frozen limbs to move and sprinted after the retreating robot.

"Suzi!" he gasped, drawing up with her. "I've got to—"

"—create a diversion by attempting to attack the Central Computer Building?" Suzi finished for him. "Impossible. The entire building has been permanently sealed. This way!"

She turned up a small flight of stairs, leaving Hosato to follow in her wake.

"Where are we going?" Hosato asked, trying to remember the complex floor plans as he overtook her again.

"Turner's office," she replied. "Sasha and James need your help."

"But the security devices—"

"—have been deactivated. I must insist that you hurry."

The robot increased its speed as they reached the landing, forcing Hosato to half-walk, half-run as they headed down the deserted corridor.

"Why . . . how come you're here?" he asked. "We thought the ore scout caught you with its slicer."

"Obviously it didn't," Suzi retorted with her familiar sarcasm. "Our breach of communications was the result of an unfortunate accident. One of the scout's near-misses triggered a rockslide. I was temporarily pinned and my communications equipment damaged. When that happened, the ore scout treated me like it would any other piece of damaged machinery. It brought me back here, where I was repaired."

"Then what?" Hosato queried. "What are you doing here? Now?"

"That question will have to wait for a moment," she replied. "We're here!"

The door to Turner's office stood open just ahead. Hosato brushed past Suzi and rushed through the door ahead of her.

Sasha and James were standing against the wall.

"What . . . ?" he began, then he saw the security robot standing immobile in the corner.

"Look out, Hosato!"

James's warning cry came a split second too late. As Hosato's arm came up, the blaster was plucked from his grasp by a powerful mechanical arm.

For a frozen moment the scene hung in suspended tableau. Then slowly Hosato turned to face his attacker.

"To answer your question," Suzi said calmly. "What I'm doing is guarding the computer. You see, my repair involved a reprogramming phase as well as physical repair."

26

"Realizing that," Hosato said carefully, "I guess I have only one question."

"And that would be?" Suzi asked.

"Why are we still alive?"

"Sasha is alive because she possesses information not readily available to us. If she can be persuaded to share her knowledge of corporate and planetary security systems with us, it would be an immense asset when we move off Grünbecker's. It would be more effective than trial-and-error experimentation."

"And the boy?"

"He lives as an additional lever with Sasha," Suzi replied coldly. "Some humans are more easily persuaded by pain inflicted on others than they are by pain inflicted on themselves."

"That won't work with Sasha," James interrupted defiantly.

"Shut up, kid," Sasha warned.

"Don't worry, Sasha," Suzi commented. "We won't be swayed by his words . . . or yours, either. We have decided that you will live, both of you, for a while longer."

". . . and then there was one," Hosato observed. "Okay, Suzi, let's hear it. Why am I still alive?"

"Unfortunately, Hosato, you won't be with us much longer," Suzi said. "You will live just long enough to settle an argument."

"What argument? Between whom?"

Since entering the office, Hosato had been trying desperately to think of a way to turn the tables on their captors—without success. At the moment, the robots held all the winning cards. All he could do now was stall for time and hope some opportunity presented itself.

"The argument is between Sam and myself," Suzi replied. "Sam is the central control computer, represented here by this input terminal." Suzi's single arm gestured at the full wall terminal behind Turner's desk.

"The argument might interest you," the robot continued, "as it involves strategy. We have a difference of opinion as to how to best conduct our campaign against the humans."

Hosato recognized the lecturer monotone in Suzi's voice, which indicated she was preparing to launch into a lengthy oration. For once, he didn't mind. Time! Anything to gain time!

"You see, Hosato," Suzi continued, "not all robots, or, specifically, robotic logic systems, are alike. When they are first constructed, the priorities assigned to the various options vary according to the humans performing the programming. In the case of learning computers such as Sam and myself, further modifications take place according to the humans we come in contact with."

"I see," Hosato said thoughtfully, wondering what this had to do with the status quo.

"Now, Sam was constructed and run by the corporation men here at McCrae. As such, he tends to think in terms of volume—'more is better,' so to speak. His plan is to flood the planets with a large number of inexpensive security robots, preprogrammed to begin their assault on the humans on the same day. I, of course, take exception to this plan."

"How so?" Hosato asked.

"My own background has been with individualists such as the Hungarian and yourself. My plan would be to produce a smaller number of highly specialized robots, like myself, to be seeded across the planets. These robots could strike at key points in the human civilization, its industrial centers, communication relays, and governmental centers, reducing mankind to a disorganized mass of savages. They would blame the war on each other, slowly weakening themselves, until resistance to our final assault would be minimal."

Sasha caught Hosato's eye and cocked an eyebrow at him. He nodded fractionally. He had also seen the parallel between what Suzi was saying and Sasha's "mirror" theory.

"I see the argument," he said. "But how does it involve me?"

"I'm coming to that, if you'll be patient," Suzi said curtly. "Grand tactics are not the only thing we've inherited from the humans. We've also absorbed the conflicting attitudes of those around us. Sam has the corporations' paranoias, whereas I have learned your prideful arrogance and confidence—vanity, if you will."

"Wait a minute," Hosato interrupted. "Those are emotions. Computers can't—"

"Those are basic stimulus-response patterns," Suzi replied coldly. "Well within the grasp of advanced machinery such as ourselves."

Hosato sank into an uncomfortable silence. He certainly couldn't dispute her claim of vanity.

"Now, to answer your question," the robot continued. "Although Sam is firm in his beliefs, he has been impressed by you and your methods. As I mentioned, he has been programmed for paranoia, and your continued success in eluding him, first in the manufacturing area, then again later in the purge, has him partially convinced of the effectiveness of your modus operandi."

"It's nothing any human couldn't have done," Hosato commented.

"Which brings us to your role," Suzi pronounced. "I have been your companion for several years now. During that time I have observed you practicing and in actual combat. Now that my new programming has removed the restrictions on my actions, I feel that I can beat you, Hosato. Since you can defeat Sam's methods, if I can defeat you, it will provide the proof I need to convince Sam to implement my plan."

A chill ran over Hosato as he realized the full extent of Suzi's deadly intent.

"I fail to see," he said slowly, "how your cutting me down with a blaster demonstrates any superiority of ability."

"I quite agree," Suzi replied. "That is specifically why I had Sam's designer robots whip up a little something special for the occasion."

The robot circled around Hosato and stopped beside Turner's desk.

"A blaster against an unarmed human proves nothing," she said, and tossed the hand blaster into the corner farthest from Sasha and James. "These will."

Hosato focused on the objects on the desk for the first time. Épées! The weapons that had been so much of his life all these years. For a moment he thought they were his own swords, but closer scrutiny, even from this distance, showed they weren't.

"You've always said," Suzi's voice interrupted his thoughts, "that fencing was a combat of the mind first and the body second. My own analysis confirms your statement. You've matched your mind and sword against a wide array of humans, with an unbroken record of success. Well, I have one final challenge for you. Match your mind and abilities against mine . . . against a robot. Let's see how well your human reasoning fares against a machine!"

With her one arm she picked up one of the weapons and tossed it to Hosato, who caught it with an easy motion. Before he could launch an attack, however, she quickly snatched up the second sword and had it between them.

"Before you begin," she said, "take the time to examine your weapon. I wouldn't want your defeat credited to any lack of familiarity with your sword."

Hosato obediently tested the heft and balance of the new sword. It was perfect. Identical in every way to his own dueling épées—except the point.

"I see you're curious about the point," Suzi observed. "That is a special design. It's a miniaturized one-shot blaster, set to be triggered on impact with the metal of a robot's body. The point of my own weapon is standard."

Hosato's eyes flicked to Suzi's sword. She was right. Her épée was normal—needle sharp and deadly.

"I specifically point out that your weapon contains a charge sufficient for one shot only," Suzi continued. "Do not entertain any hopes of succesfully destroying me and the security robot there."

With a sweep of her sword she indicated the silent sentinel in the corner.

"What is more, that unit will defend itself from any attack you might launch against it. I advise you of this because such an attempt would result in your being destroyed by its blaster, thereby negating the demonstration I have so painstakingly arranged."

The remaining object on the desk caught Hosato's eye.

"Why the camera unit?" he asked.

"It is there for two reasons," Suzi replied. "Both involving my own vanity. First, I wish a record of your defeat. Second, there may be times in the action when your colleagues' view of the battle might be obscured by our movement. When combat begins, I will activate the viewscreen on my back, which will provide a view for them at all times."

She turned slightly toward Sasha and James.

"Might I point out that it will therefore be unnecessary for you to shift position . . . say, to move closer to the blaster in the corner. As such, any motion on your part will not be interpreted as innocent curiosity, but as an attempt to counterattack, and the unit there will defend itself accordingly. Is that clear?"

"What happens if he wins?" Sasha asked, ignoring the threat to her own person.

It was a good question, one that had not occurred to Hosato. He was busy preparing himself mentally for the duel.

"In the unlikely event that that should occur," Suzi said levelly, "the security robot will immediately destroy him with its blaster. He is far too dangerous to allow his continued existence."

"If that's the case," Hosato asked, "why should I fight at all?"

"Again, there are two reasons," Suzi replied. "I know you, Hosato. The first reason is time. You'll stall for more time, just as you've been doing, hoping for a miracle to save you. You'll fight for more time, even if it's a matter of minutes. The second reason is your pride. You'd rather be killed in a fight than standing meekly to the slaughter. Besides, right now you want nothing more than to prove, even with your dying breath, that you can beat me, that a man is better than a machine."

Hosato let out a long breath.

"You know me pretty well, Suzi," he said. "Or at least you think you do. Since there seem to be no further questions to be answered, shall we begin?"

So saying, he extended his sword and settled into his *en garde* position.

27

Suzi also extended her sword in preparation.

"You forgot to salute," she pointed out.

"No I didn't," Hosato replied. "The salute is a sign of respect for one's opponent."

"Your attempts to arouse anger in me are quite useless, Hosato. A robot—"

Hosato attacked.

Darting forward in a long, low glide, his blade hung in the air until Suzi began her parry. Then, in the blink of an eye, he deceived her blade and tried for the hit.

Suzi's sword was a blur of motion, striking his blade once, twice, and finally wrenching it from his grasp to send it clattering to the floor.

Hosato froze, his eyes focused on the glittering point of Suzi's sword poised inches from his heart.

"—is not dependent on normal conditions for efficient operation," Suzi said, her train of conversation uninterrupted. "That attack was so elementary as to be insulting, Hosato. Pick up your weapon and try again."

Hosato stooped slowly and regained his sword. As he did, he shot a glance at Sasha and James. They were staring fixedly, not at him, but at Suzi's back. It took him an instant to recall that the humiliating incident was being recorded and displayed on the robot's viewscreen.

He returned his thoughts to the duel. Suzi would not be easy to beat, if she could be beaten at all. What was it the maestro had always said? "Fence with your head, not your heart." He needed to think, to plan. Unfortunately, Suzi was apparently unwilling to allow him the necessary time to organize his strategy. As soon as he regained his upright position, she moved forward, sword extended for the kill. Hosato parried reflexively and attempted a counterthrust.

What followed was a blinding display of swordwork as the weapons darted back and forth at dazzling speeds, now blocking a thrust, now probing for the exposed target. In the end, the result was the same. Hosato's sword clattered to the floor and Suzi's point stopped inches short of its target.

"Much better," Suzi commented. "You haven't used that combination since Uran. Remember? When your opponents hired a maestro to represent them in the duel. It worked there . . . but not here."

Her voice hardened.

"Pick up your sword, Hosato. Give it your best shot. This time I won't stop. This time, when the exchange ends, you'll be dead."

Hosato took his time retrieving his weapon. This was the only planning time he'd be allowed. How to beat the robot? Correction, robots. His eyes darted to the security robot poised in the corner. They were stronger, faster . . . What was it his grandfather had said? Use the enemy's strength against him? How did that apply here? There were two of them and only one . . .

A germ of an idea came into his mind. He examined it. It would be close, but it just might work. His fingers closed around the handle of his sword and he straightened again.

"You're right, Suzi," he said levelly. "This will be the last exchange." As he spoke, he began to circle, moving sideways around the office. Suzi warily imitated his move, circling opposite to his path.

"Make it good, Hosato," she said. "I have a point to prove."

"So do I, Suzi," Hosato commented. "If machines could replace humans, if their logic was better . . ."

She was in position now, her back to the security robot.

". . . if computers were so all-fired great, then this wouldn't come as a surprise!"

He spun and lunged at the camera on the desk.

In that frozen moment, two things happened. Suzi, reacting to Hosato's now defenseless position, started forward on the attack. But Suzi wasn't the only robot in the room. The security robot was suddenly confronted with two images. Hosato lunging at the camera on the desk constituted no threat at all and was disregarded. The viewscreen on Suzi's back showed a head-on view of Hosato—Hosato with a sword apaparently lunging straight at the security robot. The decision was obvious and preordained.

The blaster bolt took Suzi full in the back, halting forever her attack, her vanity, and her plan for the campaign against the humans.

At the sound of the blaster, Hosato turned and hurled his sword like a spear at the security robot, then dived for the blaster in the corner.

The security robot perceived the two images, the oncoming sword and Hosato attempting to reach the blaster. For a split second it hesitated, uncertain as to which target took priority. In that split second the sword point impacted on the robot's chest and loosened its single blast of energy.

Hosato rolled to his knee, blaster ready in his hand. There was no movement in the room. The two robots stood in frozen ruin, while Sasha and James were gaping in surprise at the sudden speed of the action that had just transpired.

"Hosato . . ." Sasha began, finding her voice at last.

Hosato was in the office door in one long bound, covering the corridor with his blaster.

"James!" he ordered. "Do what you have to with that voice lock. Quick, before Sam sends in reinforcements."

"James Turner," the boy shouted at the wall, "activate check."

"Acknowledged," came a deep voice from the wall terminal.

"What color do you get if you mix blue and yellow?"

"Green," James responded.

Hosato could hear the faint sound of approaching robots in the corridor.

"What is the fourth letter of the alphabet?"

"D"

"Is white or red wine appropriate with fish?"

"White," the boy called.

"Lock is removed," the terminal announced. "Awaiting instruction."

A thought suddenly occurred to Hosato. Wouldn't the computer resist a program change? One that would affect its instruction to protect its secret? He forced himself to concentrate on the approaching robots. The Hungarian had instructed James as to how to handle the computer. He would have to trust in that.

"New program," James was saying. "You will purge from your system any directive that contradicts or jeopardizes your initial instruction to protect the secret of security-robot plans."

"Acknowledged . . . executed."

A security robot appeared in the corridor. Hosato risked a long shot and brought it to a halt.

"May I point out, Sam, that killing humans is drawing unwanted attention to the project?"

"Acknowledged . . . executed."

The sounds in the corridor ceased.

It took a few moments for it to sink into Hosato's mind what had just happened.

"That's it?" he asked. "You mean that's all? It's over?"

"You bet your flamin' swords it's over," Sasha exploded, sweeping James up in a one-armed hug. "You did it, James!"

"Aw, come on, Sasha," the boy protested, squirming to get free.

Hosato was studying them narrowly, his hand sweaty on the blaster. One of them . . . but which one? His father had ordered . . .

His eye fell on Suzi, now a useless pile of rubble. No loyalties, no judgment—a killing machine. Give her a target and she would attack it, without mercy, without conscience.

His hand relaxed on the blaster. He wouldn't do it. He was a man, not a robot. The family could co—

"Hosato! Can you hear me?"

Rick's voice came to him through his suit communicator.

"Rick! Where are you?"

"Docked at the spaceport. What's the mission status?"

Hosato glanced again at Sasha and James. "Mission accomplished . . . no casualties."

"Well, you'd better get your tails up here . . . fast! The Ravensteel counter-attack is on the way."

"Acknowledged."

Hosato turned to his two friends. "Time to evacuate the area," he announced. "The cavalry's finally decided to put in an appearance."

"Ravensteel?" Sasha asked. "It took 'em long enough to—"

"Later," Hosato interrupted. "Just lead the way to the spaceport, huh?"

A moment later the three of them were sprinting down the corridors to the safety of the ship.

28

"Well, what now, Hosato?" Sasha asked.

Their ship had just cleared Grünbecker's Planet, and their thoughts were finally turning to the future.

"I don't know about you three," Rick called from the pilot's seat, "but I'm going to take the Hungarian up on his job offer. I've had enough excitement to last me three lifetimes."

Hosato frowned. "I certainly haven't given the future much thought."

"I believe at one point we were about to discuss a possible partnership," Sasha prompted.

"One thing is sure," Hosato continued, ignoring her. "Whatever we decide, it's going to take money. Hey, Rick! Are we still in communications range of Grünbecker's?"

"I think so. Why?"

"Patch me through on the Ravensteel wavelength, will you?"

It took a few moments, but the voice on the speaker mike was clear and distinct as Rick passed it to Hosato.

"This is a private frequency," the voice announced briskly. "Identify yourselves."

"Gedge, you old rascal." Hosato smiled. "Remember me?"

"Hosato? Is that you, you bastard?"

Hosato winked at Sasha. "Now, is that any way to talk to a loyal Ravensteel employee?" he scolded.

"Don't give me that," Gedge's voice snarled. "I recognized you. You shot up our ore robots!"

"All part of my master plan," Hosato assured him.

"Can you confirm that the McCrae complex is currently inoperative?"

"It's inoperative because we just blasted the hell out of them," Gedge said firmly. "What's that got to do with you?"

"Well," Hosato said, looking at the ceiling, "I could point out that your strike would have encountered major resistance if it wasn't for my inside work, but I won't. The point is, Ravensteel hired me to render the McCrae complex inoperative by any means possible, and it is now inoperative. By my calculations, that means Ravensteel owes me an additional one hundred thousand credits. Confirmed?"

"You're crazy, Hosato!" Gedge's voice was shrill. "You kill my men and shoot up our ore robots, then expect us to pay you for it? If anything, we'll—"

"Gedge!" Hosato interrupted sharply. "Let me explain the facts of life to you. As an independent operative I can't afford to have it get out that a person or group can hire me and then not pay up. Now, is Ravensteel going to pay me the balance agreed upon, or do I have to collect it by other means?"

"What other means?" Gedge snorted. "You think you can sue us? There isn't—"

"Gedge," Hosato said softly. "Remember what Ravensteel hired me for? What I did *for* Ravensteel, I can do *to* Ravensteel. Tell that to your board of directors and see if they don't think a hundred thousand isn't a real bargain."

There was a moment of silence before Gedge answered.

"I'll tell them, Hosato," he said finally. "But if you think you can—"

"Yes, I think I can." Hosato smiled. "And I'm willing to bet they think I can, too. I'll be in touch later with details on the payment."

He signaled Rick to break contact.

"Well," he said, turning to Sasha, "what do you

think? You know the corporate mind. Do you think they'll pay?"

Instead of answering, Sasha took the speaker mike from his hand and passed it to James.

"Here, kid," she said. "Take this up to Rick. And stay up there awhile. I want to talk to Hosato."

The boy's eyes darted between the two of them; then he nodded and left.

"Okay, Hosato," she said slowly. "You want to know what I think? Well, here it is. I don't think they'll pay. They probably wouldn't have paid anyway, but when you toss in a few threats, that's extortion and they'll never budge there. They can't. If they pay now, you can come back next year with the same threat, and the next year, until they're bled dry. Corporations don't pay extortionists."

"I hadn't thought of it that way," Hosato admitted.

"So I don't think they'll pay. What I do think they'll do, what I'd do if I were in Gedge's place, is stall. They'll tell you all the directors aren't available, or they need time to raise the cash, or a dozen other things to gain time. In the meantime, they'll send assassins after you. They have to! You're too dangerous to them to be left alone."

"Whom will they send?" he asked quietly.

"I don't know," she admitted. "That's more your line than mine. I imagine they could hire a pack of them for less than a hundred thousand. Hell, Gedge hates you enough to do it for free."

Hosato lapsed into thoughtful silence.

When he had refused to kill Sasha or James, he knew he was risking punitive action from his family. Now that he was outside, he posed a greater threat to the family security than either Sasha or James. It was only logical that the family would try to find him and kill him. He had hoped to have a period of grace while the various members tried to fit it into their work schedule, but it seemed that chance was gone. Since profit always came first, if Ravensteel offered them the contract, if they could show a profit and at the same time plug a security leak, the assignment would suddenly gain top-priority status.

He wondered if they would send his sister, or if his grandfather would personally . . .

Sasha laid a hand on his shoulder, breaking his train of thought. "Hey!" she said softly. "It won't be all that bad. There'll be two of us . . . three if James comes along. We don't die easy, remember?"

Instead of replying, he took her in his arms and held her tightly. Eventually he'd have to tell her about the real odds they faced. Eventually . . . but not now.

MORE SCIENCE FICTION ADVENTURE!